THE MASTER

OF

HULLINGHAM MANOR

A Novel

THE MASTER
OF
HULLINGHAM MANOR

A Novel

BERNARD WENTWORTH

Edited and with an introductory essay by
Gina R. Collia

NEZU
PRESS

Published by Nezu Press
Queensgate House,
48 Queen Street,
Exeter, Devon,
EX4 3SR,
United Kingdom.

This edition published 2023
Editorial material and introduction © Gina R. Collia 2023
The Master of Hullingham Manor first published by Digby,
Long and Co. Ltd., 1897.

ISBN-13: 978-1-7393921-6-1

In the interest of preserving the original text, it has not been altered. The punctuation and spelling of the original have been maintained, and the original formatting has been used wherever possible. Only very minor publisher errors in the original text have been silently corrected.

CONTENTS

The 'Phantom Recital' of
Eleanor Bateman Dashwood

by Gina R. Collia

When I began looking into the true identity of Bernard Wentworth, I had only one tiny tidbit of information to work with. In 1899, in the 'Welsh Gossip' column of the *South Wales Daily News*, it was claimed that the gentleman who wrote *The Master of Hullingham Manor* was in fact a lady. The author, according to Mr D. R. Morgan of Dinas Powis, was the daughter of Mr and Mrs Dashwood of Gwynfe, a small village in Carmarthenshire.[1] She was known amongst locals as 'Sister Norah', and, on account of her 'ready and kind disposition to render any aid within her power to anyone in need', she was 'exceedingly popular and beloved'. Unfortunately, as Mr Morgan also claimed that the author was the wife of the renowned actor Wilson Barrett, which she certainly was not, his information appeared unreliable. But it was a lead to follow—the only one I had—so I followed it.

I discovered that there was indeed a Dashwood family living in Gwynfe at the time that the 'Welsh Gossip' column appeared. James Edward Bateman Dashwood (1833-1905) and his wife Anne (née Anne Mildred Fowler, 1839-1923) had been living at Gwynfe House, in the parish of Llangadock, Carmarthenshire, since about 1893.[2] James Bateman Dashwood was the fourth son of Vice-Admiral William Bateman Dashwood, of Rosiere in Lyndhurst, Hampshire (who was unfortunate enough to have his right arm blown off during the capture of the French frigate *La Pomone* in 1811). Anne

Bateman Dashwood was the granddaughter of Walter Butler, 1st Marquess of Ormonde. And James and Anne did indeed have a daughter: their only child, Eleanor—a name often shortened to Norah—Louisa Rachel Bateman Dashwood.

Following D. R. Morgan's revelation in the *South Wales Daily News*, there appears to have been no further attempt to reveal the true identity of the writer Bernard Wentworth to the public at large. The names Wentworth and Dashwood did not appear together in print again until 1905, by which time the former was linked with an entirely different profession.

Prior to his retirement in April 1881, James Bateman Dashwood worked at the Foreign Office for thirty years; he served as précis writer and then private secretary to his cousin Lord Malmesbury, and he worked under Lord Beaconsfield and Lord Salisbury.[3] He died from pneumonia at his home in Freshford, Bath, on 11 February 1905,[4] and, being a person of some note, his death was reported in the local newspapers. The *Western Daily Press* report, along with a brief outline of his professional career, included a list of the chief mourners at his funeral; amongst them was his daughter, who by that time was going by the name of Mrs Bernard Wentworth.[5]

The following year, in November 1906, a memorial tablet for James Bateman Dashwood was installed in the north transept of St. Michael's Church, in the village of Lyndhurst in Hampshire. *The Hampshire Advertiser* described the unveiling and dedication of the 'handsome brass tablet of novel and artistic design' and reported that it was erected by the 'daughter of the deceased gentleman': Mrs Bernard Wentworth.[6] These newspaper reports regarding James Bateman Dashwood's funeral and memorial confirmed that his daughter, Eleanor, and Mrs Wentworth were one and the same person. And further research revealed that the latter name was more than a nom de plume; it was an alias used by Eleanor in daily life—one of many, as it turned out.

Eleanor Louisa Rachel Bateman Dashwood was born on 21 April 1861 at 3 Gloucester Terrace, Westminster, London.[7] By the time she was ten years old, her family had moved to Wentworth House on Elgin Road, in the civil parish of Weybridge, Surrey; the household included a cook, two housemaids, and a groom.[8] It was in Surrey that she met Manfred William Robert Brotherton (1854-1904), seven years her senior and the son of John William Brotherton, gentleman and late lieutenant of the 11th Hussars.[9] Eleanor and Manfred were married on 1 December 1880 at St Mary's Church in the parish of St Marylebone, Westminster;[10] Eleanor was nineteen years old. The couple honeymooned in Paris then returned to England to take up residence with Manfred's mother, by then a widow, and sister at The Firs in Esher, Surrey.[11] The couple's only child, Irene Frances Mildred Brotherton, was born on 1 February the following year.[12]

The marriage was not a happy one, and on 4 September 1883, less than three years after their wedding, Eleanor and Manfred separated. On 11 December 1883, Manfred filed for divorce.[13] Eleanor counter-filed, and the case came before the Right Honourable Sir James Hannen in the Divorce Division of the High Court in June 1885.[14] Eleanor was accused of committing adultery with three men: Rev. Francis Sumner, formerly a curate at Cobham, Surrey; William Shannon, a Dublin solicitor; and Henry Pryce Hamer, an amateur actor. In response, Eleanor accused Manfred of adultery and cruelty.[15]

According to Manfred, Eleanor was given to flirting, lying, and confiding in the servants (who gave evidence against her). He claimed that Eleanor's relationship with Rev. Sumner had begun just a year after her marriage, that she had received love letters from William Shannon after a visit to Ireland in the summer of 1883, and that in January 1883 she had gone with Hamer to a hotel in Ryde, where the two had had adjoining rooms.[16] Manfred testified that, at first, Eleanor had admitted to committing adultery with Hamer, but when confronted by her parents she had called them 'old fools' for believing such a story. In the hope of reconciliation, he said, he had taken Eleanor to Switzerland. However, while there he had accused her of flirting with two German gentleman, and in response she had struck him so hard that his nose bled and the skin was scratched from his face. Eleanor then left her husband in Switzerland and returned to her parents, who were by then living in Wales. Manfred claimed that he had made several visits to see her in Wales and had offered to take her back, but she had refused him.[17]

Elizabeth Anne Wilson was a ladies maid within the Brotherton household from 1881 to 1883 and gave evidence against her mistress during the divorce proceedings.[18] According to Miss Wilson, Eleanor had admitted to her that Reverend Sumner was the father of her daughter (whom she loved less than the cat), that the reverend had showed her indecent pictures, and that she had been 'naughty' with Shannon.[19] Eleanor had also confided in her maid that she had passed herself off as Hamer's wife during a visit to Ryde, that Manfred intended to challenge Hamer to a duel, and that she wished her husband would be killed so that she could marry Hamer and go on the stage.[20]

The Brothertons' gardener, Henry May, testified to having seen Eleanor kissing Rev. Sumner in the garden, and another servant, Annie Stedall, claimed that she had seen the reverend enter her mistress's bedroom.[21] But for the most part, the statements made by household staff concerned various fancies that Eleanor had shared with them about her relationships with her co-respondents; they provided no evidence to prove actual, rather than imagined, adultery. Elizabeth Wilson admitted that Eleanor had a habit of 'romancing'; she had once claimed, without there being any truth to her story, that she had been engaged to the Duke of Portland.[22]

Eleanor testified that Manfred was cruel and physically violent, and that his ill treatment of her had begun immediately following the couple's marriage. She claimed within her petition that, whilst on honeymoon in Paris, Manfred had bought French books of an 'indecent and disgusting character' and had asked her to translate them for him, that in January 1881 he had pushed her with such force that she had fallen and struck her head against the fireplace fender, and that later that year he had forced her from the billiards room, 'knocked her down and put his foot upon her.'[23] She accused him of drinking too much and using offensive language, and she claimed that, on 29 January 1883, he seized her 'by the hair and threw her out of bed', causing her to 'bruise her head'.[24] While they were in Biarritz, Manfred had hit her about the ear so hard that she had lost her hearing temporarily, and he had committed adultery; he had had relations with 'some woman' who was unknown to him and had 'thereby contracted a venereal disease.'[25]

Mr Clarke, QC, acting on behalf of Rev. Sumner, described Manfred as 'watchful and jealous'.[26] Eleanor, prone to 'romancing' about men who were not her husband, was the most inappropriate choice of wife for a man with a suspicious nature. Eleanor denied all of her husband's allegations, but the jury found her guilty of adultery with Henry Pryce Hamer. Manfred, likewise, denied his wife's allegations; at least, he did so in writing prior to his appearance in court. Once in court, however, he admitted that he had pushed his wife, pulled her hair and slapped her on the ears, but he insisted that 'he was never guilty of what could be called "ill treatment." '[27]

He also admitted to sometimes drinking too much; on one occasion, he had been found drunk on a bench outside a hotel in Biarritz, and 'his clothes might have been dirty.'[28] The jury found that he was not guilty of cruelty or adultery. Based on witness testimony, Sir James Hannen concluded that Eleanor must have been 'in the habit of telling untruths'.[29] He granted a decree nisi and awarded costs against Hamer.

The newspapers were not kind to Eleanor. She was described by reporters as 'a very vain and frivolous young woman' who 'was possessed with the morbid idea that every man was in love with her'; as a result, she had 'deliberately forfeited all claim to affection and respect.'[30] Manfred, on the other hand, was congratulated for having rid himself of his wife, with whom married life must have been 'an intolerable torture'.[31] With her marriage dissolved, Eleanor's future, it was surmised, was 'not an agreeable prospect'.[32]

Manfred was given his decree absolute on 12 January 1886.[33] He was also given sole custody of the couple's daughter. Five months later he remarried. His second wife, Guilia Dealtry (née Guilia Williams Wynne), was also divorced. In June 1885, as Manfred was in court seeking to end his marriage to Eleanor, Guilia was filing for her own divorce.[34] When the couple married, on 26 June 1886,[35] Manfred's divorce settlement was still in the process of being finalised, and Guilia's decree absolute had been granted only four days earlier. It is not possible to know for certain whether or not Manfred entered into an affair with Guilia Dealtry while still married to Eleanor, but, unless his courtship of his second wife lasted only a few days, he most certainly began a relationship with Guilia while she was still a married woman.

When Manfred married Eleanor, he settled upon her an income of £500 a year. After the decree absolute was granted, the settlement was altered by the court, and Manfred was required to provide Eleanor with £200 a year, paid quarterly, for the remainder of her life, with the condition that she 'should lead a chaste life'.[36] By the autumn of 1892, Manfred had stopped paying her allowance on the basis that the condition had not been met, and in May 1893 Eleanor was back in court, suing her former husband to recover arrears of £150.

After the divorce settlement was drawn up, in the summer of 1886, Manfred hired private detectives to observe Eleanor in her daily life.[37] During this new court case, he accused her of 'having misconducted herself with unknown men at a coffee-house in Paddington, and also with Mr. Wilson Barrett', the well-known stage actor,[38] thereby violating the condition of the settlement. In response to Manfred's charge of impropriety, Eleanor argued that she had become delusional as a direct consequence of 'people, as she believed, following her about';[39] she had become hysterical, suffered from hallucinations, and had 'got the idea into her head that she was the wife of Mr. Wilson Barrett'.[40]

Numerous letters were introduced as evidence of Eleanor's impropriety, including a long correspondence with a Mrs Watts, in which she had repeatedly represented herself as Wilson Barrett's wife. In one letter, she had described how the actor sat up 'till nearly twelve o'clock waiting for his bread and milk', as he 'would not have it from the cook', preferring to wait for Eleanor's return.[41] In another she had claimed to be the actor's understudy, 'ready to go on at a moment's notice should he fail.'[42] Signing herself 'Norah Barrett', Eleanor had invited people to visit the Carmelite church to hear her husband sing (Barrett couldn't sing a note) or to the theatre to see him act.[43] And she had written notes on his behalf, which she signed 'Good-bye, Wilson'.[44] It was revealed that, in addition to 'Mrs. Wilson Barrett', Eleanor had used several other aliases; she denied using the name 'Norah Lee', but she admitted that she had assumed that of 'Violet Warrington', under which she had gone on the stage and recited in private theatricals.[45]

The newspaper reporters had a field day with the story, some referring to Eleanor as a madwoman in their columns while the case was still ongoing. The reading of her letters in the courtroom had to be paused at times to allow the laughter of the audience to die down. And the experience was so upsetting for Eleanor that her cross-examination had to be brought to a halt when her nose began to bleed.[46]

Wilson Barrett himself was in America at the time and could not attend court, but his brother George and his manager, Giovanni Pollini, gave evidence, testifying to the fact that there was not, and never had been, any intimate relationship between Eleanor and the actor. Pollini had never seen Eleanor before, and the first he had heard of Barrett being mixed up in the affair was when 'a bill for a trousseau was received from Madame Elise'.[47] Eleanor's father gave evidence during the court case; his daughter had told him that she was engaged to Wilson Barrett, and he had dismissed the whole business as 'an hallucination and a farce.'[48]

After evidence of Eleanor's alleged impropriety was presented, it was clear to all—though Manfred still claimed otherwise—that she was delusional; she was neither engaged nor married to Wilson Barrett, and there had been no improper relationship between the two. Whether or not Manfred's behaviour had been, as Eleanor claimed, the sole cause of the deterioration in her mental health, he had certainly had her followed for years—he himself had followed her on at least one occasion[49]—and she had felt persecuted. Eleanor explained that she had 'got into a terrible state' as a result of her husband's cruelty and had been 'turned out of house after house' due to his private detectives following her about.[50]

Manfred admitted in court that his detectives had never found Eleanor and Wilson Barrett 'in communication'.[51] With regard to the allegation that Eleanor had behaved improperly with 'other men' at a coffee-house in Paddington, witnesses gave evidence of her movements which proved her innocence, and Manfred 'did not persist in those charges'.[52] Mr Kemp, QC, acting for Eleanor, argued that shortly after the divorce settlement deed was drawn up—more than seven years earlier—Manfred had sought 'to get rid of what he considered a burden' and had hired private detectives to help him do so.[53] It is important to note here that Manfred was a wealthy man who had no need to work; when he died in 1904, he left an estate worth more than £51,000, which was a considerable sum of money at the time (worth in excess of £4,000,000 in current money).[54] He sought to deprive Eleanor of an income he could well afford to pay, and he 'pursued a system of persecution and annoyance by reason of which [Eleanor's] mind became affected.'[55] His detectives—he made use of multiple—made no attempt to hide their interest in Eleanor; every time she settled at new lodgings, Manfred's men made sure that she was forced to move on again.

Manfred Brotherton 'failed entirely to establish any relations' between Eleanor and Wilson Barret,[56] and when the court case concluded, on 13 May 1893, the special jury, without retiring, found in Eleanor's favour. Lord Chief Justice Coleridge said that Manfred's allegations of impropriety were 'not supported by any kind of evidence', and he awarded Eleanor the £150 arrears she had sued for, plus costs.[57] Manfred had no choice but to continue paying her allowance.

We have, from the reports of this court case, our only brief physical description of Eleanor: 'She is a lady of pleasing features, about middle age, and wears spectacles.'[58] The people of Penarth in the Vale of Glamorgan, Wales, where she had lived in lodgings during the six months prior to the court case, found 'Mrs. Wilson Barrett' to be 'an entertaining and exceedingly musical companion wherever she went, albeit excitable and hysterical at times'.[59]

Following this second court case, Eleanor appears to have ceased using her former husband's name; she also managed to avoid appearing on a single census return from that point on. During the case, she claimed that she acted and recited in private theatricals, that her stage name was Violet Warrington, and that she had appeared in a performance of *As You Like It* at the St. James's Theatre in 1890;[60] outside of the reports of the court case, I can find no mention of her under this name. At some point between May 1893 and the beginning of 1897, Bernard Wentworth came into being. At the same time, to the people of Gwynfe at least— according to Mr D. R. Morgan in the 'Welsh Gossip' column of the *South Wales Daily News*—Eleanor continued to claim that she was the wife of Wilson Barrett. Mr Morgan's information regarding 'Sister Norah' turned out to be quite reliable after all.

In 1896, Eleanor's only child, Irene, died at the age of fourteen. She was buried in St. Andrew's Church in Cobham, Surrey, on 8 May.[61] In all likelihood, Eleanor had not been allowed to see her daughter since her divorce in 1885; Manfred would most certainly have denied access on the basis that Eleanor posed a moral threat to an innocent, impressionable young girl. There was never any suggestion made that Eleanor had attempted to maintain any sort of relationship with her former husband, and Manfred, though he had had his former wife watched for years, and had followed her himself, appears to have had no direct contact with her.

On 22 May 1896, two weeks after his daughter's funeral,

Manfred filed for divorce.[62] He accused his second wife, Guilia, of committing adultery with James MacLaren Smith, and asked for damages of £10,000. Solicitors for both parties were heard, and on 10 July 1896 Manfred's petition was dismissed.[63] Guilia, it turned out, was not to be got rid of quite so easily as Eleanor. So, two years later, Manfred Brotherton—the man who claimed to be so concerned about impropriety—was still married to Guilia when, on 17 February 1899, his mistress, a domestic servant called Augusta Hampton, gave birth to his son in the town of Dinan, in Côte-du-Nord, France.[64] When Manfred returned home from France with his new family, Augusta was presented as his 'wife'; she declared herself as such on the 1901 census.[65] Guilia didn't die until the following year, on 23 May 1902.[66] Manfred and Augusta were married exactly one calendar month after Guilia's death, on 23 June 1902.[67]

In June 1897, Eleanor was living in a cottage on Penally Terrace in Boscastle, Cornwall. She wrote to the *Western Morning News* to complain about 'the utter carelessness with which the relics of historic interest are being sacrificed to the modern landowners' passion for gold.' The coastline, she explained, was being destroyed to 'procure stone for building purposes.' Could nothing be done, she asked, 'to save the Coast of Cornwall from destruction?'[68] The letter was signed 'Bernard Wentworth'. Shortly after she wrote this letter, her novella *The Master of Hullingham Manor* was published by Digby, Long and Co. Ltd. It appears to have been the only book she had published.[69]

Carlos Hullingham, the master of Hullingham Manor, is a handsome devil: physically perfect but morally bankrupt. He is society's darling, 'But behind the sensuous charm of exterior there lurks the spirit of a fiend, ruthless in its cruelty and malice.' When his first wife, Adelaide Hullingham, becomes an annoying obstacle that stands between him and his happiness—that is, marrying a pretty young girl called Mora Alderson—he decides to get rid of her. He locks Adelaide up in the 'vaulted room', a brick structure within the manor garden, forcing her to live there in isolation, without heat, without proper meals, and with no access to her children.

'My prison was damp, and like a mildewed dungeon…The only window was a small square opening in the northern wall, devoid of glass, through which the wind blew and the rain splashed, and in all the years I spent there I never saw the sun. There was no fireplace in this deadly vault, in which the cold penetrated night and day. Its only furniture, an iron bedstead, a wash-hand-stand, and a single wooden chair. No books were allowed to me, no work, no clock by which to count the passing hours.'

Once free of Adelaide, Carlos Hullingham marries Mora, but in time his second wife becomes as much a burden to him as his first wife was. He has a new mistress, the young actress Reine Donati. So, Mora must be dealt with too. But Mora is determined to expose her husband's wickedness, and she hatches a clever plan to reveal his true character to the world during a 'Phantom Recital'.

Like Eleanor, Adelaide married a deceitful man who behaved as a devil in private while presenting the front of a respectable gentleman to the world at large. Like Eleanor, poor Adelaide was tormented by her husband and became unstable as a consequence. Like Manfred, Carlos succeeds in duping society. Like Manfred, Carlos wants rid of his wives because he has willing replacements waiting in the wings. And like Manfred, Carlos is a wealthy man who cruelly seeks to remove his wife's income to leave her without the means to live.

Though, as far as we know, there was no 'vaulted room' or

asylum in Eleanor's actual history, *The Master of Hullingham Manor* is certainly based upon her own life and experiences. In the novella, Adelaide Hullingham chose to record her story, and the truth about her husband's cruelty, within a written 'confession'; in real life, Eleanor chose to expose her own husband's cruelty by writing a fictionalised account of it in *The Master of Hullingham Manor*. The novella was published only a year after Manfred's failed attempt to discard his second wife, when he was most likely already in an intimate relationship with the woman who would become his third and last wife. As to the name of the book, Hullingham Manor was a fictional location, but Hullingham House was very real. Located at 38, Marine Parade, Brighton, it was a guesthouse at which Eleanor stayed a number of times. After her father's death, she continued to visit there with her mother.[70]

Aside from being called a 'fearful and wonderful production of the approved "penny horrible" type' by the *Dundee Advertiser*, *The Master of Hullingham Manor* received very little attention.[71] According to *The Author*, two poems by Bernard Wentworth were published in the *Western Mail*: 'Tintagel, by the Cornish Sea' (29 January 1897) and 'Anti-Agnosticism' (15 January 1898). Apparently, the former ran to a second edition in booklet form, published by Messrs Weighell and Co. of Launceston.[72] A short story entitled 'Allerton Farm' appeared in the Christmas edition of the *Cornish and Devon Post* in 1897, and by February 1898 the author was working on a new book, *Anne Pentargen: Or, the Spirit of the Tor*, which was to be published serially in 1899.[73] I have found no evidence to suggest that this novel was ever published.

Following the 1893 court case, Eleanor had continued using the name Mrs Wilson Barrett during visits to her family in Wales; she also claimed whilst there to be a member of the medical profession.

Several short notices appeared in the Welsh newspapers about her visits. In May 1897, the *Cardiff Times* wrote:

> Gwynfe is just now honoured by the presence of Mrs Wilson Barrett, whose father resides at Gwynfe House. By profession Mrs Wilson Barrett is a nurse, and is known as sister Norah. She is exceedingly popular at Gwynfe, and makes herself quite at home amongst the inhabitants.[74]

In July the following year, the *South Wales Daily News* reported that Mrs Wilson Barrett, who was again in Gwynfe, had returned only recently from Australia, where she had been 'touring with her husband's "Sign of the Cross" Company.'[75] Eleanor continued claiming to be Barrett's wife until, on 22 July 1904, he died. At his funeral, amongst the numerous floral tributes there was one from Mrs B. Wentworth.[76] The adored actor was dead, and Mrs Wilson Barrett was heard of no more.

In December 1898, there was an announcement in the *South Wales Daily News* that Mr Bernard Wentworth, the poet-novelist, had joined the ranks of journalism, having been given a position at a leading Warwickshire newspaper. It was also claimed that the author had been commissioned to write the libretto for a new opera by the well-known composer Garnet Wolseley Cox.[77] Given that this information was most likely provided to the newspaper by Eleanor herself, it is impossible to say whether or not there was any truth in what was printed.

Around 1901, Eleanor's parents left Gwynfe; perhaps it is merely a coincidence that they did so shortly after Manfred and his wife moved to Wales. Eleanor moved to 11 Forester Road in Bath,[78] and her parents took up residence at The Grove in Freshford, only five miles from their daughter.[79] The first mentions of *Mrs* Bernard Wentworth appeared in 1903, within newspaper reports of meetings of the Wiltshire Anti-Vivisection Society, of which she was listed as the honorary secretary;[80] she remained in that post until 1908.[81] Then, in 1905 and 1906, the name appeared in reports of James Bateman Dashwood's funeral and memorial dedication. Also within those reports was the clue to Eleanor's new occupation.

When the brass tablet dedicated to Eleanor's father was erected in St. Michael's Church in Lyndhurst, Hampshire, 'Dr E. M. Bernard Wentworth, of London' officiated at the organ.[82] Of course, there was no *Dr* E. M. Bernard Wentworth of London. There was, however, *Mrs* E. M. Bernard Wentworth of Bath, soon to become '*Madame* Bernard Wentworth, M. Gld. O (Gold Medallist, &c.), the celebrated lady concert organist'.[83] By 1905, Eleanor, the would-be actress and poet-novelist, appears to have given up her acting and writing aspirations completely in favour of pursuing a career as a professional musician. Also, by this time Manfred Brotherton was dead. He died at his French residence in Dinan, Côte-du-Nord, on 5 May 1904;[84] Eleanor was finally free of him.[85]

In July 1907, it was reported in the *Bath Chronicle and Weekly Gazette* that Madame Bernard Wentworth was the recipient of a solid silver rose bowl 'in recognition of services as organist at various cathedrals and churches in London and the provinces' and had been engaged 'by Mr. Arthur Royd, of the Royal Albert Hall, for his forthcoming concerts in London, under Royal patronage.'[86] It is almost certainly the case that this is entirely untrue. Prior to November 1906, E. M. Bernard Wentworth the organist, whether Dr, Mrs or Madame, did not exist.

Shortly after the above report appeared, Mrs Bernard Wentworth appeared in the newspapers for an entirely different reason. In March 1907, St. Patrick's Clergy Hostel, a nursing home for poor Church of England clergy and their families, was officially opened at 6 Cavendish Place, Bath. It had been founded by the Anglo-Irish social reformer Canon William Henry Cooper. Eleanor was appointed assistant honorary secretary.[87] Local physicians were very supportive of the project; clergymen, on the other hand, 'turned their noses in the air, and buttoned their pockets.'[88] Canon Cooper, having received harsh criticism, became so agitated that his heart gave way, and his doctor insisted he give up work to save his life.[89] St. Patrick's Clergy Hostel closed, and the house and its contents were put up for auction. In her official capacity, Eleanor had hired Charles Frederick Lawday and his wife to work at the home: the former as butler, the latter as cook and housekeeper. When the home was closed, Lawday sued Eleanor for one month's unpaid wages.[90] Canon Cooper, being seriously ill at the time, could not appear to give evidence. Judge Gwynne-James adjourned the case until September, but the matter seems to have been resolved before the case returned to court.

Returning to Eleanor's musical career, in October 1907 she attempted a provincial tour, beginning at the Victoria Rooms in Bristol on the 19th of that month.[91] She played F. J. Breitenbach's pastoral fantasy *L'Orage*, complete with darkened hall, raindrops, 'mechanical thunder and lightning, hail and wind', for 'a somewhat small audience'.[92] On 12 November, she appeared at Park Hall in Cardiff, where she had 'a very good audience and a thoroughly successful evening.'[93] On 16 January 1908, she played in London for the first time, at the Æolian Hall on New Bond Street, but the reviewer for the *Globe* wasn't impressed by the mechanical effects, which were 'not entirely convincing.'[94]

When Eleanor's father died in 1905, her mother moved to 11 Forester Road to live with her. By the end of 1909, Eleanor's career as a touring professional musician had come to an end, and she was starting out on a new venture. At the beginning of 1910, mother and daughter moved to Brighton, staying first at Hullingham House on Marine Parade.[95] On 15 May 1910, a dedication service took place at 61 Preston Drove, Brighton, to celebrate the founding of a new religious society, the Christian Spiritualist Mission, and the new church of S. Michael and All Angels.[96] The house was that of Madame Bernard Wentworth, the founder, who at the conclusion of the ceremony played a postlude by Elgar on the piano.

> 'The drawing room of the House has been beautifully arranged as a Chapel, there being a full-sized altar, with a silver crucifix in the centre, lights on either side, and a picture of the Saviour. The reredos is a very impressive painting of the Archangel Michael standing upon the steps of the Throne of Heaven, and resting upon a flaming sword, above him in the clouds appearing a large black cross, with a circle of flame and a halo of lightning.'[97]

This new church had been founded to produce a form of worship in which all creeds of Christianity were blended with the purest teachings of Spiritualism. 'The service was very uplifting,'[98] hymns were sung, a collection was taken for the poor, and an address was given by Sister Hannah Ramsay, the deaconess.

By the beginning of January 1912, the society had changed its name to S. Michael's Christian Spiritual Church (S. Michael's Mission to Restore the Banished Christ), and it was holding regular meetings at Brunswick Hall, 2 Brunswick Street East, Western Road, in Hove. Madame Bernard Wentworth was now Sister Wilson Wentworth, medium and trance speaker;[99] Wilson, of course, being taken from the name of Wilson Barrett, the beloved actor.

S. Michael's offered sermons, clairvoyant circles, psychometry, materialisation, Bible reading and various classes; circles took place at Eleanor's home on Mondays. Advertisements for the church, which was renamed S. Michael's Mission, First Christian Psychic Church, continued to appear in the Brighton newspapers until the end of December 1912,[100] at which point no further were placed.

Eleanor died from heart failure, with her mother at her side, on 17 November 1914 at the age of fifty-three; she had suffered from mitral valve disease and rheumatoid arthritis.[101] She was buried four days later in Hampstead Cemetery, Camden.[102] The fittingly inaccurate funeral notice in the West Sussex Gazette read:

> 'The funeral took place, at Hampstead, on Saturday, of Mrs. Wilson B. Wentworth, founder of St. Michael's Mission, known as the First Christian Psychic Church to Restore the Banished Christ, who passed away at her residence in Wish-road, Hove, in her 55th year. Mrs. Wentworth, a Doctor of Music, was a gifted organist, and for a year was organist at St. Paul's Cathedral.'[103]

Eleanor led a very troubled life. She was abused, persecuted, humiliated and ridiculed. But she persisted to dream. She was imaginative—that goes without saying!—musical, theatrical and spiritual. She had grand aspirations; she wanted to be a great actress, writer, poet, or musician. But the reality of carrying out any of these professions fell far short of her romantic imaginings. I hope that, in the end, she found some peace in the community of her spiritualist church. I also hope that the publication of this essay—this record of her true history and exposure of her husband's cruelty—will serve, even in the absence of flowing robes and phosphorescent make-up, as the 'Phantom Recital' of Eleanor Bateman Dashwood.

Notes

1   *South Wales Daily News*, 4 January 1899, p. 4.

2   According to the *Carmarthen Weekly Reporter* (23 February 1900, p. 6), the Bateman-Dashwoods rented the house and shooting rights from Major Basset Lewis, formerly chief constable of Cardiganshire.

3   Bower Marsh and Frederick Arthur Crips, *Alumni Carthusiani: A Record of the Foundation Scholars of Charterhoue, 1614-1872. Privately printed*, 1913, p. 243. Also, *Western Daily Press*, 16 February 1905, p. 5.

4   *Weekly Mail*, 25 February 1905, p. 12, for cause of death and location. For date: *England & Wales, National Probate Calendar (Index of Wills and Administrations), 1858-1995.*

5   *Western Daily Press*, 16 February 1905, p. 5.

6   *Hampshire Advertiser*, 24 November 1906, p. 9.

7   *Westminster, London, England, Church of England Births and Baptisms, 1813-1919.* St Mary, Tothill Fields, 1861-1872.

8   *1971 England Census*, Surrey, Weybridge.

9   *Freeman's Journal*, 14 October 1839, p. 3. John Brotherton purchased his commission and was promoted from the rank of cornet to lieutenant in 1839.

10 *London, England, Church of England Marriages and Banns, 1754-1938*, Westminster, St Mary, Bryanston Square, St Marylebone, 1879-1885.

11 *Globe*, 24 June 1885, p. 6.

12 Ibid.

13 *England & Wales, Civil Divorce Records, 1858-1918.*

14 Ibid.

15 Ibid.

16 *London Evening Standard*, 25 June 1885, p. 3.

17 Ibid.

18 The newspaper reports refer to the witness as Helen or Ellen, but the census return for 1881 gives her name as Elizabeth.

19 *London Evening Standard*, 25 June 1885, p. 3.

20 *Echo*, 24 June 1885, p. 2.

21 *London Evening Standard*, 25 June 1885, p. 3.

22 *Cambridge Independent Press*, 27 June 1885, p. 8.

23 *England & Wales, Civil Divorce Records, 1858-1918*. The Petition of Eleanor Louisa Rachel Brotherton, 7 February 1885.

24 Ibid.

25 Ibid.

26 *Derby Daily Telegraph*, 26 June 1885, p. 4.

27 *London Evening Standard*, 25 June 1885, p. 3.

28 *Echo*, 24 June 1885, p. 2.

29 *London Evening Standard*, 25 June 1885, p. 3.

30 *Western Morning News*, 29 June 1885, p. 4.

31 Ibid.

32 Ibid.

33 *England & Wales, Civil Divorce Records, 1858-1918*. Brotherton v. Brotherton, Sumner, Shannon and Hamer, court minutes.

34 *England & Wales, Civil Divorce Records, 1858-1918*. Dealty v. Dealty, court minutes.

35 *London, England, Church of England Marriages and Banns, 1754-1938*, Westminster, Saint John the Evangelist, Paddington, 1867-1888.

36 Divorce settlement. High Court of Justice: Probate, Divorce and Admiralty Division, document dated 30 July 1886.

37 *Morning Post*, 15 May 1893, p. 6.

38 *London Evening Standard*, 12 May 1893, p. 1.

39 Ibid.

40 Ibid.

41 *Reynold's Newspaper*, 21 May 1893, p. 3.

42 Ibid.

43 *London Evening Standard*, 12 May 1893, p. 1.

44 Ibid.

45 *Reynold's Newspaper*, 21 May 1893, p. 3.

46 Ibid.

47 *London Evening Standard*, 12 May 1893, p. 1.

48 Ibid.

49 *Globe*, 13 May 1893, p. 7. Manfred Brotherton gave evidence that he had followed his former wife into the National Gallery, where he inspected the visitors' book to check which name she used when signing it. He discovered that she had signed 'Norah Barrett'.

50 *Reynold's Newspaper*, 21 May 1893, p. 3.

51 *Daily Telegraph & Courier*, 15 May 1893, p. 6

52 *Northern Guardian*, 15 May 1893, p. 3.

53 *Reynold's Newspaper*, 21 May 1893, p. 3.

54 *England & Wales, National Probate Calendar (Index of Wills and Administrations), 1858-1995*, 1904. When Manfred died, on 5 May 1904, his estate was worth £51,294 12s. 9d., which would be worth in excess of £4,000,000 now (using the retail price index, The National Archives, Currency converter: 1270–2017). The allowance of £200 awarded Eleanor by the court would be worth only £15,700.

55 *London Evening Standard*, 15 May 1893, p. 2.

56 *Morning Leader*, 15 May, 1893, p. 2.

57 *Home News for India, China and the Colonies*, 19 May 1893, p. 22.

58 *Reynold's Newspaper*, 21 May 1893, p. 3.

59 *Western Mail*, 15 May 1893, p. 6.

60 *Reynold's Newspaper*, 21 May 1893, p. 3.

61 *England, Select Deaths and Burials*, 1538-1991.

62 *England & Wales, Civil Divorce Records, 1858-1918*. The Petition of Manfred William Robert Brotherton, 22 May 1896.

63 *England & Wales, Civil Divorce Records, 1858-1918*. Brotherton v. Brotherton and Smith, July 10 1896.

64 *1901 Wales Census*, Merionethshire, Llanaber.

65 Ibid.

66 *London, England, Church of England Marriages and Banns, 1754-1938,* Wandsworth, Saint Paul, Battersea.

67 *England & Wales, National Probate Calendar (Index of Wills and Administrations), 1858-1995,* 1902.

68 *Western Morning News,* 7 June 1897, p. 5.

69 I have found no other novels/novellas by Bernard Wentworth. However, given Eleanor's penchant for using aliases, it is impossible to say with absolute certainty that she published no others.

70 Various sources, including *Brighton Gazette,* 30 October 1909, p. 7.

71 *Dundee Advertiser,* 29 July 1897, p. 2.

72 *The Author,* 1 March 1898, p. 272.

73 *The Author,* 1 February, 1898, p. 250.

74 *Cardiff Times,* 8 May 1897, p. 1.

75 *South Wales Daily News,* 9 July 1898, p. 4.

76 *London Evening Standard,* 26 July 1904, p. 6.

77 *South Wales Daily News,* 30 December 1898, p. 4.

78 *England & Wales, National Probate Calendar (Index of Wills and Administrations), 1858-1995,* 1905.

79 Various sources, including *The Post Office Bath Directory 1911,* as Mrs E. M. Bernard Wentworth, p. 34.

80 *Trowbridge Chronicle,* 12 December 1903, p. 6.

81 *Wiltshire Times and Trowbridge Advertiser,* 29 February 1908, p.2

82 Hampshire Chronicle, 24 November 1906, p. 9.

83 *Morning Post,* 15 January 1908, p. 1.

84 *England & Wales, National Probate Calendar (Index of Wills and Administrations), 1858-1995,* 1904.

85 Manfred Brotherton did indicate, at the close of the 1893 court case, that he would continue to pursue a charge of impropriety against his former wife. There was no further court case, but it's entirely possible that he never stopped having her watched.

86 *Bath Chronicle and Weekly Gazette,* 4 July 1907, p. 4.

87 Bath Chronicle and Weekly Gazette, 28 March 1907, p. 3.

88 Bath Chronicle and Weekly Gazette, 2 May 1907, p. 8.

89 Ibid.

90 Bath Chronicle and Weekly Gazette, 18 July 1907, p. 2.

91 *Western Daily Press*, 7 October 1907, p. 5.

92 *Bath Chronicle and Weekly Gazette*, 24 October 1907, p. 2.

93 *Western Mail*, 11 November 1907, p. 6.

94 *Globe*, 17 January 1908, p. 3

95 *Brighton Gazette*, 16 February 1910, p. 7.

96 *Southern Weekly News*, 21 May 1910, p. 10.

97 Ibid. (Also, the 'reredos' is the ornamental screen that covers the wall at the back of the altar.)

98 Ibid.

99 *Brighton Argus*, 6 January 1912, p. 2.

100 *Brighton Argus*, 28 December 1912, p. 1.

101 Death certificate for Eleanor Louisa Rachel Brotherton.

102 *UK Burial and Cremation Index, 1576-2014*. London Borough of Camden, Hampstead Cemetery.

103 *West Sussex Gazette*, 26 November 1914, p. 9.

CHAPTER I
GHOSTS

S NOW is falling heavily and silently outside, clothing trees and house and gardens in a mantle of glittering whiteness, and an ominous stillness forecasts more to come.

Midnight has struck on the grandfather clock in the hall, its chimes sounding sepulchral in the night silence.

In a carved armchair before the dying embers of a fire of logs in the oak-panelled library at Hullingham Manor, illuminated but by the lurid glow, sits the master of the house—Sir Carlos Hullingham— in a brown study.

The apartment, gorgeously furnished in an old-world style, in tapestry and antique oak, betrays the voluptuous temperament of its owner, in the Oriental perfumes, exotic flowers, and waving palms grouped here and there in artistic profusion. The floor, of polished parquet, is slippery as ice, and reflects, as in a mirror, furniture and flowers, except where it is hidden with Persian rugs and skins of Polar bears. Over the doors rich *portières* of olive plush are hung, upon which, in blue and gold, are embroidered the Hullingham arms. The windows, seen by day, are of stained glass, the leaden casements opening on to a fair prospect of wooded hills, and a mist-veiled city far below. The lights have long been all extinguished, yet hour after hour the man sits on, musing in the gloom.

Over the massive black oak chimney-piece, upon which stand antique bronzes, curios of various descriptions, and an ancient cross of beaten brass, a trophy from some ruined church in Spain, there hangs a picture, heavily framed in an oval frame of gold—the portrait of a woman.

Wondrously fair is the face in the flickering light of the fire; from the broad brow masses of red-gold hair, such as is seen in the paintings of Rubens, are drawn loosely back and pinned in a Grecian coil. Cheeks just tinged with a carmine glow; lips exquisitely formed and slightly parted; and eyes deep and fathomless, the colour of pansies after rain—eyes veiled, as it were, in a mist of tears. Oh, the sadness, a weird and haunting sadness, telling the tale of heartbreak from which she died. The portrait is that of Adelaide Hullingham, the fair dead wife of the man before the fire.

Many ghosts flock unseen in this room to-night. But one alone, if visible, would have power to move Sir Carlos, that of his dead brother, Reville Hullingham. Even the wistful face of Adelaide moves him less than the mere thought of him, whose blood stains the piano in the drawing-room.

An ancient legend in the annals of the House of Hullingham tells that on the stroke of midnight on New Year's Eve must retribution fall upon the sinning members of that name.

There have been many wicked Hullinghams, men at the sound of whose tread their women-folk have trembled. But never since the name first grew to be a name has there lived a Hullingham so deeply steeped in sin, or a man of such complex nature, as the present master of the manor.

Truly a fiend in angel's guise.

See him, as he sits before the fire, a figure with no ungraceful angle, perfect in the symmetry of form. Each limb proportioned with the sinuous grace of the tiger, each movement as he stirs suggesting the tiger's pliant motion, deadly in its fascination. A face statuesque in its clear perfection of outline, with a beauty as that of some mighty fallen angel. Eyes of a luminous blue, in which burn fires of golden glow, eyes alluring in magnetic attraction or sinister in imperious command.

As a young man his hair was of a rich brown, curling round his brow; now, at the age of fifty-five, the curls, no less luxuriant, are tinged with gray.

Born in Spain and of Spanish extraction, he inherits the latent cruelty and passion of the Spaniard, his innate chivalry, generosity, and pride.

But behind the sensuous charm of exterior there lurks the spirit of a fiend, ruthless in its cruelty and malice.

Gifted to a high degree with literary power and oratory, the books he sends forth, of high-flown idealism and spirituality, enfold him in a radiant halo of fame; and the poetic sentiment with which he clothes his language, both in his writings and daily speech, have won for him the adulations of a hoodwinked world. Unchallenged he bears upon his course, the glittering tinsel of his personality effectually concealing the inward blackness of his soul. Yet any breath which may inadvertently escape of his true character from the few persons who truly know him is voted by the idolizing world as slanderous libel. Yet twelve years ago this paragon was guilty of a series of inhuman acts of cruelty, culminating in a despicable criminal fraud, a *foul conspiracy*, by which a helpless woman was done to death, his fair wife Adelaide, whose portrait hangs in the library at Hullingham Manor.

Two persons in this world alone are cognizant of the details of this conspiracy, and of her martyrdom—for no less it was— Mora Alderson, his second wife, the present Lady Hullingham; and Janet Stirling, a hospital nurse.

Mora, whom he has long since tired of and cast upon the world, he fears more or less, aware that she has gleaned fragments of the past little to his credit.

Since he married her, bound by the ties of legality, he frets at his bonds, and by incisive cruelty essays to break her heart also, and drive her to her grave; for his affection for her is dead, the present recipient of his love—if love it can be called—a foreign actress, Reine Donati, a dark Creole woman, resembling Mora—as the lump of coal the diamond.

And yet, unknown to him, Mora Alderson, the despised, insulted wife, holds him in the hollow of her hand; for between them lies her knowledge of every detail of his crime.

Thus, at a moment that he dreams not of, Nemesis may come— retribution swift and sure.

What if, through his desertion and ill-treatment, Mora were to turn and rend him? But he laughs the idea to scorn.

'Mora, little Morie, whose love for me has stood unmoved through worlds of sorrow; Mora, my willing slave, bound to me by every tie of a passionate devotion, what need I fear from her? In spite of all my harshness, she loves me still, and would return to me at once, but for Reine. Besides, what can she know of——' And he glances uneasily around.

Fool! Even as he sits in his chair by the fire, pondering upon the dark, passionate beauty of Reine Donati's face, confident of security in Mora's love; even now, when he least suspects it, the links are forging of a retribution so terrible that ere many days have passed his sin-stained soul shall be hurled into a furnace of remorse, searching as the flames of the refiner's fire.

Dream on, poor guilty fool, dream on! Forge further plans for Mora's martyrdom, as twenty years ago you planned the murder of Adelaide. Soon shall the duped world's eyes be opened. Soon shall its idol be revealed in all his blackness, stripped of his shining tinsel.

Dream on! The hour is fast approaching for Adelaide's avenging, when the finger of scorn and contumely shall point you out. Murderer and hypocrite! Woe to you then, Carlos Hullingham! Woe in the hour of retribution!

*   *   *   *   *

The mystic veil between mortal vision and the spirit-world is for a brief space lifted for the reader, and in the gloom of the vast apartment the deepening shadows are thickly peopled with the spirits of the dead.

Each as it comes and goes, appearing and vanishing into gloom, looks at the figure in the chair and sighs; but if he feels their presence he pays no heed.

At last a spirit comes to him, a fair, pale spectre, and stands beside his chair. He starts, and turns his head from side to side, scanning the darkness; but his eyes are blinded that he cannot see; yet a burden seems upon him, as when he tore at the coffin-lid which hid her form.

'Kitty!' he murmurs, 'little Kit!'

The spirit smiles; the waving tendrils of her hair brush against his cheek as she bends to imprint a kiss upon his brow.

He shivers and heaves a smothered sigh, for it seems to him as though she called him.

'Father! father dear!'

He cannot bear to think of her: his fair young daughter Katherine—little Kit—who, in spite of his sins, pitied and loved him. Muttering an exclamation, he rises abruptly, pushing the heavy hair from his brow.

'It must be the wind; there's no one here, yet I could have sworn I heard Kitty's voice.'

He crosses to the windows, tears aside the tapestry curtains, and throws wide the casements. No sound without; silently, softly, fall the downy flakes of snow; no breath of wind stirs the leafless branches of the trees, or the ivy round the windows.

A cold shiver seizes him, and he looks around, passing his hand across his eyes.

'Strange! my nerves must be unstrung,' he mutters uneasily. 'I thought I heard my—my brother Reville calling to me; this room seems full of ghosts to-night.'

He re-fastens the windows, and is drawing to the curtains, when again the voice sounds on his ear:

'Carlos! Carlos!'

A mighty trembling shakes him, and the drops break out upon his brow, but with a courage born of despair he cries aloud:

'Reville Hullingham, if you are here, stand forth.'

'Carlos!'

'In God's name I command you, stand forth!'

From the fast-deepening gloom a flimsy shape is formed: a figure clothed in diaphanous mist; a thin, ascetic face, with large, reproachful eyes, which, like those of the picture on the wall, bear in them a haunting sadness and the trace of a terrible fate. The features, though not handsome, yet bear a striking resemblance to those of his brother, Sir Carlos. A short beard and a drooping moustache, of chestnut hue, cover the lower part of the face.

'Carlos, I am here.'

Hullingham sinks on to a chair, and hides his face. In the gentle presence of the spirit, which seems but the reflection of a boundless sorrow, he feels no fear—nothing save remorse for his share in his brother's death.

'Pity!' he cries. 'Forgive!'

6

'Forgiveness is from God; look to Him. Follow me.'

In the light of a mystic luminance from the spirit's form they pass into the great hall, with its stained-glass windows and broad oaken staircase, where many a time young Edonè, Mora's child, would spring from stair to stair in the days gone by. Crossing the hall, they pause before the drawing-room door, a stately salon, furnished in the style of Louis XVI., in old rose, blue, and gold. Of the two great windows, one opens on to the garden, the other into a beautiful conservatory, now disused, but bearing traces of richly-grouped chrysanthemums of varied kind and colour; of drooping passion-flower, and yellow creeping roses, withering or dead. Here too, against the wall, from floor to roof, stands the now empty cage where once dwelt Edonè's squirrels. Now only straw and broken nuts remain to tell their tale.

Into this room, for six long years, no foot has passed till now. The furniture looks ghostly in its sheeting covers, and the dust lies thick upon the floor. As the spirit stops before this door, a cry escapes from Hullingham's lips:

'Not here! not here! I dare not enter here.'

But ruthlessly the spectre answers: 'Follow me!'

With shaking limbs and face of chalk, the wretched man follows his ghostly guide, and they pass within the room. Here all his children lived and laughed and played, with Mora, radiant in her happiness, the centre of his home. Here, on the Persian rug before the hearth, with his bricks, played the little Spanish *caballéro*, Edonè. Here, by the piano, where now he stands, died his brother, Reville Hullingham. Now all are gone—most are dead, the rest scattered, and Mora cast upon the world, deserted; for he has wearied of one whose love was so unchanging; and in her place reigns an actress, whose life will bear no scrutiny.

Hullingham shivers as these ghosts of the past flock to his memory, and there comes to him a sickening sadness. The phantom points to an inlaid davenport, at which his wife Mora sat to write her letters. Carlos advances and opens it. On the top of some old letters, and an endless litter of memoranda of little import, he sees a newly-written document.

'Read!' says the spectre.

Tearing it open in the mystic light, Hullingham reads as follows:

'CARLOS HULLINGHAM,

'I know your secret. I have kept it up to now because I loved you. Your own acts have killed that love, and it is dead. Look for no mercy at my hands; you will find none. On *New Year's Eve*, in accordance with the record of your house, at *midnight* your crime will be exposed.

'For eternal peace look to your God in time; on earth you can expect but retribution.

'MORA ALDERSON.'

The paper falls from his hand and flutters to the ground, as with a wild cry the wretched man stretches out his hands towards his brother's spirit; but the spectre vanishes and he is left alone in darkness in the ghostly room.

CHAPTER II
MORA'S HOME

IN a poorly-furnished top floor of a small lodging-house, in one of the cheapest outskirts of London, lives Mora Alderson, Lady Hullingham. In spite of the years of sorrow that have passed over her, a tidal wave of Carlos Hullingham's tyranny, she is handsome still, with a shadow of her once brilliant beauty. Her hazel eyes, which change to blue and gray, and even black, in some lights, are fixed upon the houses opposite, as she stands by the window in her shabby black dress.

In the dismal street below bits of straw and paper and other refuse are blown in eddies, by a gusty north east wind, along the dirty, snow-trodden pavements into the gutters of this London slum. Noisy, unkempt children scream at their play, their shrieks mingling with unmusical cries of costers and milk and cat's-meat men in their daily rounds.[1]

A tap at the door rouses her at last; and a woman's voice calls: 'Mora?'

'Is that you, Lucy? Come in.'

She turns, and a wan smile distorts her wasted face, and a hacking cough shakes her frame, weakened by illness, suffering, and want.

'Mother sends you this, dear, if you will accept it;' and Miss Heywood lays a brown-paper parcel upon the table. 'There's a

---

[1] Costers: short for costermongers, men who sell goods, especially fruit and vegetables, from a cart or barrow. Milk: milkmen. Cat's-meat men: those who sell chopped meat for cats from a cart.

cake—the one you like—a pound of tea, and some mushrooms Milly sent.'

'Lucy, you—your kindness kills me. I can bear harshness to any amount, but kindness such as this—no, don't kiss me!' and her voice trembles, and she presses her hands to her aching eyes, into which, in spite of her emotion, no tears will come.

'Mora, don't let the world and trouble make you hard, dear!' says Miss Heywood gently. 'But there! what's the good of talking like this? Sophistry's all very well, but it won't heal a breaking heart or feed us when we're hungry. See here, too: I've brought you those letters you want. I have been thinking of what you told me last night, and I think you are justified in frightening Sir Carlos, and if these letters will help you which he wrote to me last spring, you shall have them; but I want them back—they are the only power I have to hold over him, in case he injures you. How you can love that man after the way he treats you——'

'Love him?' cries Mora, a lurid fire of passion burning in her eyes; 'I *hate* him!'

Lucy shivers.

'I can scarcely believe you are the same woman I knew at Brighton and at Hullingham Manor,' she says; 'or, for the matter of that, last year, at Earl's Court. You were sad and miserable then, poor child! but you were not like this.'

Mora laughs bitterly.

'I was different then,' she says. 'I was cowed, my spirit broken, but I loved him still. It was sufficient for me to know that it was his hand that inflicted the suffering upon me, for me to bow in silent submission. The memory of the Carlos I loved, a memory bitter-sweet, was with me still, for there were gleams off and on, even through his harshness, to remind me of the man I loved with so passionate an adoration. But now, by his own actions, he has killed that love, crushed out the last remaining spark. *Kensington* was the straw which broke the camel's back—*Kensington* and the Scarborough Hotel, when he allowed that foreign woman, Reine Donati, openly to insult me in a public place. But for those two episodes, I might never have become what now I am, Carlos Hullingham's most deadly enemy.

'Oh, if you could read my heart!' she goes on after a pause; 'could feel one atom of the agony I suffer, consumed by a raging fire within, a burning furnace never quenched in its relentless fury night nor day, its flames devouring all the Christian charity which once was mine! Lucy Heywood, if in the final reckoning I am lost, then mayhap the world shall know that the foot which stamped me down to hell was that of Carlos Hullingham, the—the—oh, words fail me wherewith to designate him!—consummate murderer, hypocrite and liar!' and in a frenzy of passion she throws herself face downwards upon the shabby horsehair sofa, writhing, and tearing her handkerchief to shreds between her teeth.

Lucy Heywood stands petrified, uncertain what to do; and for some time the silence is unbroken save by Mora's tearless sobs and the noises in the street outside.

'Mora! Mora! poor child, in mercy, cease!' she cries at last, kneeling upon the floor at Mora's side. 'Much more of this will end in madness. Madness? what am I saying? Mora, listen here! Mora, listen to me, dear: never, never act in any way which could lead your husband to believe his treatment could drive you mad!'

Lady Hullingham raises herself slowly from the couch, in her eyes a still smouldering fire—her manner quiet, with an ominous calm. She pushes the dark hair from her eyes, and in a metallic tone, 'Mad?' she says. 'No, I am not mad yet, whatever I may be if this goes on.' Then, suddenly changing her tone and manner: 'No! Carlos Hullingham shall never lay that unction to his soul; besides I have work to do.'

'What do you mean?' asks Miss Heywood. She does not like the look on Mora's face, which augurs ill for Hullingham.

'Never mind,' says Mora, biting her nails, and swaying her body sideways to and fro.

'Why did you marry that man, Mora?' Lucy asks, after a long silence.

Lady Hullingham turns her head, and gazes intently into her friend's face for some moments without answering.

'I married him because I loved him,' she says at last—'if *marriage* it can be called.'

'What do you mean? Surely you are his wife?'

'I may be,' Mora replies listlessly. 'When it suits Sir Carlos' purpose, he says I am, but really I cannot tell.'

'But you were married in the church? Tell me about it again, if you can, Mora.'

'Oh, you know the circumstances well enough. We were married under *pseudonyms*, as he desired to keep the marriage a secret for a time. I loved him so intensely, I never dreamed he had a motive for deceiving me, so I yielded on his promise to proclaim it, and acknowledge me publicly, as soon as he was able. Thus, only a few privileged friends, yourself amongst the number, ever knew a marriage had taken place. On May 29, 1889, as you know, the ceremony was performed at *St. Cyprian's* Church, Maida Vale.

'After this, at Hullingham Manor, my life was one long dream of joy—such joy, Lucy, as I had never thought to know. Adelaide's children loved me, and we were all as happy as the day was long. At night when his arms were around me, my head upon his breast, and by the soft glimmer of the little ruby lamp I read the love he bore me in his eyes, we talked of happy plans for years to come, when Edonè should be grown to the glorious manhood his boyhood promised, and Kitty should be my right hand in my social and household duties. And then, how when old age should come upon us, we should live again in our children's children, till at last, hand-in-hand, we should pass into that land where there is no more parting. That, Lucy, was my life at Hullingham from 1889 to 1892. A striking contrast between then and now! what think you?' and she laughs a bitter laugh. 'Now the grass grows thick on Edonè's grave, and the snow lies deep on Kitty's, while *I*—well, I am here. Kensington first, now here! There is little fear of monotony in a life like mine: driven from my home, an outcast, to make room for a newer toy; thrown into the workhouse, when almost starved to death, through lack of means to support myself—all this in order to drive me to my death, as once before poor Adelaide was driven, by despair! And yet I live! When I am dead, Carlos will marry Reine Donati, and I—I shall be forgotten.'

'Oh, Mora, Mora! how do you bear it all?' Miss Heywood cries, the tears coursing each other down her cheeks. 'But he will be punished, dear——'

'Yes, he will be punished. On New Year's Eve the blow will fall.'

'What *do* you mean? Mora, don't look like that; you frighten me! What do you mean?'

'*Retribution!*' and Mora's eyes flash with a sombre flame.

'Retribution?' echoes Miss Heywood almost inaudibly. 'How?'

'I hold Adelaide's *Confession.*'

'I know. You have had that some years now. It only tells the terrible story of her martyrdom, poor hapless woman!'

'It tells that, fourteen months before she died, Adelaide Hullingham regained her sanity! It tells that Carlos Hullingham knew

13

it! It tells that, for a sum of money given to him by Carlos, that inhuman scoundrel Braiser concealed the fact and kept her there, until from a broken heart she died.'

'My God, Mora! this isn't true. It can't be true?' Miss Heywood cries, still kneeling upon the floor at Mora's feet. 'What could be his motive for so diabolical a fraud? Why did he do it, Mora?'

'In order—to—marry—me.' And she buries her face, grown ashen, in her hands and shudders.

Miss Heywood starts to her feet.

'Mora! No, no, I'll not believe it. It *can't* be true! You——'

'It *is* true.'

'But you, surely you——'

'No; I knew nothing. I only knew what Carlos told me, that she was mad. I was with her at the last. Together, he and I, we went to the asylum, summoned by a telegram to the effect that she was dying. When we arrived there, Carlos would not face his victim—at the time I wondered why—but paced the garden to and fro, until they told him that she was dead. My arm was round her when she breathed her last, yet not one word did she utter of the cause of her death. I only learned the truth from her confession two years ago, when, as you know, it was sent to me by a nurse named Janet Stirling, her attendant at the asylum, who became her friend.'

'Then, this nurse knew——'

'Yes; but Adelaide persuaded her to withhold her knowledge, so as to spare Carlos, whom to the last she loved. Sister Janet, who had grown to love her, consented upon one condition.'

'And that?'

'That Adelaide should write a full confession of the truth to *me*, withholding no detail of her martyrdom; and this, for Carlos' sake, she did.'

14

'And this, that you allude to, is the *Confession?*'

'Yes.'

'Mora—don't—don't tell me any more! And you loved this— this devil incarnate—this Carlos Hullingham? Mora, how could you?'

'Yes; and she loves him still!' says a quiet voice at the door.

Both women start up. In the earnestness of their conversation they had not noticed the gentle tap, and the visitor had entered.

'Frank!'

'Mr. Hullingham!'

'*You*, Frank! *You here?*' falters Mora; 'I thought you were in Australia!'

'So I was till I was sent for.'

'But—but, how did you find me here?'

'Rowlands wrote to me claiming my assistance on your behalf, in my father's name, who———'

'Laurence! Oh, Frank, if he had lived! Laurie! Laurie!' and, sinking upon the couch, she covers her face with her hands and sobs aloud. They are the first tears she has shed since the episode of *Kensington.*

'It was the worst day in your life, Mora, the day when Mr. Laurence died,' Miss Heywood says, sitting beside her, while Frank Hullingham crosses to the window, and stands looking out, a big lump in his throat. 'That was a *man* and brother!'

'You're right, Miss Heywood,' young Hullingham cries, turning towards them. 'Aunt Mora married the wrong brother when she wedded Uncle Carlos. My father said so many a time. He loved her too, but with a quiet, unassuming devotion that ministered to her needs in a way which———'

'Frank, if you love me, speak not of Laurence!' cries Lady Hullingham, starting up, and dashing the tears from her eyes as she crosses to the window. 'I cannot bear it! Smarting as I am

15

under Carlos' ill-treatment, I dare not think of Laurence. His loss to me——'

'Aunt Mora!' exclaims her nephew, his honest plain face aglow with pleasure; 'do I understand that you had a deeper feeling for my father than——'

'Frank, do not speak of it, I implore you! I am Carlos Hullingham's wife; do not tempt me to unfaithfulness to him, even in one thought.'

'What a magnificent woman she is!' thinks the young man admiringly; then, to his aunt, he says:

'But see how he treats you! What a tyrant he is! See the shameless woman he sets above you, in your home, casting you upon the streets!'

'Yes, Frank; I know all that,' says Mora wearily. 'Still, he is my husband, and though my love for him is dead, killed by his own actions, I will not stain my wifehood by one thought of Laurence, of whom, though dead, to think would be a sin.'

'Miss Heywood and Frank exchange a glance in silence, and Lucy nods and noiselessly claps her hands. Frank moves over to Mora at the window.

'You do love him, then—his memory, I mean. Aunt Mora, if you could only forget——'

'Stand back!'

In Mora Alderson's eyes a strange fire burns; her face is pale, her gesture commanding, as she waves him back, her whole figure endowed, as it were, with a new majesty.

'Frank Hullingham,' she says, 'how dare you come here to remind me of—of the dead, at a time when I am crushed and friendless; and when I warn you that the memory of my husband's brother holds sin for me, you seek to force from my lips a confession I would rather die than make, even to you—his son! You taunt me, because you think I dare not claim an honest woman's right to cast that foreign reptile from my home; that, remembering my past, I could not cast a stone. You are wrong;' a burning blush mounts to her brow, and her voice trembles. 'It is true that, through my love for your uncle, Carlos Hullingham, I became myself a sinful woman; but I sinned from love alone. I was young; I was ignorant; and, led away by Carlos Hullingham's persuasive tongue, ready to yield my life, if necessary, for him I loved, I sinned. Had I received a sound religious training in my youth, things might have been different: I had not; but through suffering I grew to understand. Now my sin has been condoned by marriage; of the sin itself I have long ago repented; and as a wife, Frank Hullingham, I stand redeemed, and, by God's grace, pure. You come to me, and tempt me to infidelity, in thought, to Carlos Hullingham. Go! I never wish to look upon your face again;' and with faltering steps she moves to the fireplace, where the few poor lumps of coke, which her scanty means afford, give out but little warmth.

The young man takes up his hat and stick in silence and walks to the door; but, with his hand upon the handle, turns and glances back to where his aunt is standing, so regal even in her sorrow and her dress of poverty.

Shamefacedly he returns, and stands behind her.

'Forgive me, Aunt Mora,' he stammers; 'I was wrong; I'm sorry. The thought of my Uncle Carlos drove me to it. I can't bear to see you here in this wretched place, and all so different to what it used to be. Say you forgive me, Aunt Mora, and that for the—for my father's sake you'll let me help you over the present difficulties?'

Mora turns and holds out her hand.

'I suppose I must forgive you, at least this time,' she says with a dreary smile; 'but never speak to me again of—of your father, as you did just now. Your kind offer of help I—I'm afraid I must refuse, Frank, tempting as it is to me to feel that someone cares sufficiently for me to offer help. Still, I cannot accept money from Laurence Hullingham's son. Though I were starving, yet must I still refuse. I think you will see I am right.'

For some time there is silence, as the young man toys with a knife on the table.

'Yes,' he says at last, 'I suppose you are right; I understand the motive which prompts you to refuse, and I honour you for it, Aunt Mora—still, I'm sorry. This cloud will pass by some day, I think, and you and Uncle Carlos will be friends again, and we shall have the good old times once more at Hullingham. Cheer up; one never knows what the future's got in store!'

'No, Frank,' Lady Hullingham answers sadly; 'that can never be. Come, let us talk of something brighter than my doleful story. Tell us of your life at Sydney; that will, at least, be more enlivening.' And he does.

CHAPTER III
'KENSINGTON'

T HE reader has doubtless been puzzled by the numerous allusions to Kensington. If he would understand the future actions of Mora—Lady Hullingham—we must glance back to a period five months ago.

In a road off the Kensington *High Street* there stands a straggling, red-brick building, enclosed within high walls and giant iron gates, guarded by a porter's lodge.

This building is the Kensington Workhouse.

Five months ago, before the iron gates, which were opened to admit them, there stood a man and a woman.

The man was attired in an Inverness cape, red-lined, wore a soft hat, and carried a silver-mounted stick.

The woman, looking scarcely more than a girl, was neatly clad in shabby black, and genteel poverty was plainly legible in every line of her weary face. Her eyes were dull with unutterable despair, and the red flush on her face spoke of the shame she felt in being there.

The man was Carlos Hullingham, the woman his wife—Mora Alderson.

Incredible as it seems, the man has ground her down to this. Into her home at Hullingham Manor he has introduced a shameless woman, an actress—Reine Donati—who nightly played a leading part at the *Imperial Theatre* in London.

Until he should give her up, and return to his lawful wife,

Mora had left her home, retiring into a boarding-house near to the British Museum, where every day she worked.

After many attempts to force her to return, her husband threatened to stop her allowance if she persisted in the course she was pursuing, but she still held firm. Then every indignity that spite could conceive he heaped upon her, thinking to drive her back, in spite of Reine Donati, but in vain.

One day, in what she deemed a passing fit of kindness, he gave her a cheque, and sent her with her friends, the Heywoods, to the *Pier* Hotel at Scarborough for a week.

They had been there about four days, when one afternoon, as Mora and her friends were drinking tea in their private room, in walked Sir Carlos Hullingham, accompanied by the Creole actress, Reine Donati. Mora turned first red, then pale, as with quiet dignity she rose.

'This, Sir Carlos, is an honour I did not expect and scarcely appreciate. I am pleased to see you, of course; but either Miss Donati or my friends and I must leave the room. Which is it to be?'

Hullingham, finding that the onus of action rested upon him, coloured deeply, then shrugged his shoulders with an uneasy laugh. The actress looked from one to the other with contemptuous scorn.

She was a fine-looking woman, this Reine Donati, young, with a rich, swarthy complexion and ruddy colour. Her dark eyes were deeply set under strongly-marked brows, and her masses of coal-black hair she wore coiled closely round her head. Handsome she was not, yet there was an indescribable something about her personality which, though coarse, attracted men of Hullingham's mould.

As her husband gave no reply to her question either in speech or action, Mora signed to her friends, and they left the room.

That evening, as they were going down to *table d'hôte*,[2] Hullingham begged his wife, for appearance's sake, to permit Miss Donati to sit at her table. At first she indignantly refused, but on Hullingham whispering something in her ear she flushed deeply, and at last consented. The dinner passed off in a silence of pained constraint, except to the actress, who looked at the ladies and around the room with a vulgar stare and on her lips a satirical smile.

Almost everyone in the room recognised her, and to most persons present Sir Carlos Hullingham was known by sight, and some had heard the scandal of his behaviour to his wife, and their thoughts were scarcely flattering either to him or Miss Donati.

As dessert was brought, more champagne was opened, and whether the wine was more than the Creole girl could stand, or whether what followed was an exhibition of her natural vulgarity— who can tell?—but in a loud voice, with mocking laughter, she commenced to criticise both Mora's dress and person in a slighting manner, ending in an open insult, which was overheard by all present in the room. A murmur of 'Shame! shame!' was audible on all sides, and everyone turned to gaze at their table.

Lady Hullingham looked blankly at her husband, her eyes filling with tears of humiliation, but he was smiling at the Creole's drollery, and neither by word nor gesture essayed to stop her tongue. Signing to her daughter, Mrs. Heywood rose, and taking Mora's arm—for she seemed stunned—they left the room.

That night they left for London, Hullingham and the actress remaining at the hotel.

Two days after her return to town, Lady Hullingham received a curt note from her husband informing her that he had stopped her

---

2 *Table d'hôte*: a dining table set aside for residents of a guesthouse.

allowance from that day, and that she must either return to him upon his terms or starve. Her answer was as short:

'Give up Miss Donati, and I return at once; otherwise I decline.'

From this day began a time of slow torture for the wretched girl. She left her boarding-house, and took a cheap room in a poor but respectable street off the Earl's Court Road, where she lived upon her 'savings.' The day came, however, when this well ran dry; then she was well-nigh starving. Day after day passed, and she looked at the bare larder in her lodging cupboard. All of value, of dress or jewellery, she had pawned for bread whereon to live, and there was nothing left that would fetch a penny piece. With wild eyes she sat down, and stared at the empty shelves in horror. Starvation! Then there came to her a brilliant thought born of despair. She would make herself as respectable as she could, and call upon her friends. The chances were she might be asked to tea or luncheon. At first she turned from the idea with loathing. It seemed so mean to prey upon one's friends. But hunger triumphed, and in this manner she managed to exist for a few weeks longer. A brave face she made before her acquaintances, many of whom said, 'How well you look! Come again soon.' And she did. With the exception of these stray meals, and a slice of bread with a glass of milk in the mornings, she had nothing to eat. Yet, wet or fine, she tramped each day to the Museum, hoping that when her work was done—a translation for a publisher—she would earn a few pounds; but it was not to be.

Meeting with some friends one day at the Museum, they asked her to return with them to dine and go to the theatre. She accepted eagerly, poor girl! The thoughts of that dinner were more than she could resist. After the play, they parted at the theatre door, and she told them she could get an omnibus at Piccadilly.

As she passed the door of the *Café Monico*, smiling to herself at her little deception—for she was penniless, and must walk home—she came face to face with Sir Carlos Hullingham standing at the entrance of the restaurant in evening dress and smoking a cigar. She stopped, growing faint and pale, and begged his mercy, saying she could hold out no longer; that, if he did not help her soon, she must really starve, or apply to the law. He only laughed, mean cur! He knew too well that this faithful woman would die before she dragged his name before a court of law. He knew that, in spite of all, she loved him still; but her 'obstinacy,' as he termed it, staggered him. He thought she would have given in long ago.

Rain began to fall in heavy drops, and the growl of thunder startled her, and she said she must hurry on. She asked him to give her the fare of an omnibus to Earl's Court, yet, in spite of the heavily-increasing rain, he refused.

'Stay, though,' he said. 'You needn't get more wet than necessary. Take this'—handing her his umbrella—'I can drive home. Excuse me now; I have friends, and Miss Donati awaits me for supper, so good-night, Mora.'

'Have you no pity, Carlos? Don't send me away like this, alone!'

'You have your remedy,' he answered curtly, turning into the *café*, and Mora tramped on in the lightning and rain.

Holding her husband's umbrella, poor loving fool! she pressed her lips against the non-sentient handle.

'Oh, if he would but love me once again!' she cried, and kissed his umbrella as the dog kisses the hand of the master who beats him.

Illness followed the drenching she received, added to the want of nourishment and the misery she had endured, and for weeks she wandered in the delirium of fever. When she rose from her bed, to her dismay she found herself in her landlady's debt for seven weeks' board and rent, and not a *sou* wherewith to meet the bill.[3] Reluctantly the good woman said she must leave, but allowed the debt to stand till Mora earned the money with which to pay. Thus, weak and ill, she found herself upon the street penniless.

Remembering that she possessed a fairly good voice, nightly she dragged her steps to the Bayswater squares, where she sang for pence before the houses. In this way she earned sufficient to keep body and soul together for another week; but feeling her strength to be failing, and another illness imminent, she wrote to her husband begging him to meet her at the Pro-Cathedral the following day at noon.

He came, and she placed the lodging bill and the state of affairs before him.

'So you are coming to your senses, then, at last—eh, Mora?'

'That depends upon you,' she answered wearily. 'While that woman remains at Hullingham Manor I shall never return. I would die rather. Give me sufficient to feed myself and pay for a respectable lodging over my head, and I will ask for nothing more.'

'There's the workhouse. You needn't starve.'

'*Carlos!* You would send me *there?* Are you man or devil?' and she laughed hysterically. 'They wouldn't take me while you live to protect me.'

'Oh yes, they would, if *I* placed you there as *Emma Alders*, a pauper. Few know of our marriage, and as I am on the Board of Guardians, no questions would be asked. At any rate, it's better than starvation, I should say.'

---

[3] *Sou:* an old French coin of low value, a very small amount of money.

'You—you *fiend!*' she hissed. 'And this is the man upon whom I have lavished a soul's deep love for twenty years, for whom I sinned! Ye gods! ye gods!'

Finding that he refused to help her, and that starvation indeed must be her lot if she defied him, at last she yielded; and that very day, under the name of *Mrs. Alders*, a pauper, he placed her in the Kensington Workhouse. And to the superintendent who received her he said:

'Be kind to the poor woman; she has been ill, I think. Should you desire to communicate with me at any time about her, you have my address at Hullingham Manor.'

'Perfectly, Sir Carlos; and rest assured that Mrs. Alders will be well cared for here. It's curious the prejudice the poor folks have against the house. It's better than the streets, any way, eh?'

'*I* should say so,' said Hullingham, and he laughed. Then, turning to Mora, who seemed dazed and turned to stone: 'Well, good-bye, Mora—Mrs. Alders. I trust you will be comfortable here.'

Lady Hullingham looked at him with withering scorn, and turned away without vouchsafing him a word.

'God!' she cried upon her bed that night, 'that I could have loved that man! Oh, the shame! the shame!' And she wept as if her heart would break.

Gradually her sobs grew less and less, and finally stopped. And then it was that the hemlock poison of bitterness entered into her soul and turned her love to hatred—relentless, implacable hatred, that boded ill for Hullingham, and bid fair to end in his undoing.

CHAPTER IV
PATIENCE HULLINGHAM

ONE afternoon, about a week after Frank Hullingham's visit, Mora is startled by the announcement that a stranger desires to see her, but will not give her name.

A quiet woman makes her appearance, attired in slight widow's mourning—a woman of about forty, looking younger. she is not pretty, but a *piquante*, *spirituelle* face, with fluffy fair hair and fine eyes, redeems her from plainness.[4] A Manner of shy reserve suggests an effect of 'stand-offishness' which is misleading. Her voice is soft and distinctly refined, yet an indefinite 'something' about her personality savours of the middle class.

'Am I addressing Mrs. Alderson?' she asks with a pretty smile, and a red spot on either cheek.

'Yes, I am Mora Alderson,' Lady Hullingham says courteously; 'but I have not the pleasure of knowing you, I think. Please sit down;' and she drags a chair to the fire.

'You are Mora Alderson?' the visitor goes on with a peculiar wistfulness in her look and manner as she regards Mora with an intentness which is embarrassing. 'In other words, you are Lady Hullingham, Sir Carlos Hullingham's wife. Ah! you start because I know your name. We are in a way acquainted, although we meet face to face for the first time to day. I am Reville Hullingham's widow!'

Mora starts violently, and colours painfully.

---

[4] A *piquante*, *spirituelle* face: an attractive, refined face.

'You—you are *Reville's widow*, and you can come to *me?*'

Mrs. Hullingham mistakes her meaning, and fancies her presence is unwelcome, and she rises nervously.

'I—I came to you, Lady Hullingham, because I heard you were in trouble, and I hoped you would not turn from me when you knew my name; I see I was mistaken, therefore I will intrude myself no longer upon you. I came because in the past, when your husband, Sir Carlos, disowned his brother Reville for marrying me, a farmer's child, you, Lady Hullingham, were kind, and supplied us with funds from your private purse, when we must otherwise have starved.'

Mora's heart beats wildly, and now, impulsively, she takes her sister-in-law's hands.

'Patience, my dear; stop! You have misunderstood me quite. You thought that because you are Reville's wife your presence was unwelcome; it is just the other way. I was so taken aback that, after the infamous way in which Carlos treated you and Reville, you could bring yourself to come to me, his wife.'

'You were kind to me, Mora; I'm not a woman to forget a kindness.'

'It is good of you to come,' cries Lady Hullingham, making Patience sit down again, and kneeling by her side. 'I am truly grateful to you for your friendship, at a time when I am friendless, and an—an outcast. How did you learn my address?'

'From Frank Hullingham. As you know, he's in England; he ran down to see me two days ago, and mentioned having been to you. He told me of Sir Carlos' infamy. I'm not surprised, after the way he treated his brother Reville, and his first wife, Adelaide.'

'He can be very cruel sometimes,' says Mora limply.

'Well, now, my dear, as to the object of my visit. If you can overlook the fact that I am only a farmer's daughter, and not your equal in rank and station, will you give up this lodging here, and come and share my home at Rottingdean? I'm poor, as you know, so I can't offer you the luxuries of Hullingham Manor; but you may be sure of an honest welcome in a homely cottage, as of my sisterly love. Will you come?'

Lady Hullingham rises, staggered. With both hands pressed to her brows, she stands for some moments in silence.

'And you say this to me—to the wife of the man who so insulted you? Patience!' she cries hoarsely.

'No; I offer my home to Mora Hullingham, the woman who befriended me and my dead husband. Will you come?' she asks again.

'God bless you! Yes, I'll come;' and Mora throws her arms round Mrs. Hullingham and kisses her.

'That's all right. I'm glad I came to-day.'

'Stay, though; I'm afraid I can't come. I forgot,' Mora says in confusion; 'I've no money.'

'Well, what of that? What's enough for three's enough for four, I reckon?'

'Then, I'll come if I may stay with you till I can get something to do—teaching, or something by which to make a living; for Carlos has stopped my allowance, and I am penniless, except for what I earn by sewing for the poor people in this neighbourhood—a shilling or two a week, to keep me alive.'

'Well, that's all done with now, Mora; and as to teaching, I dare say there's plenty to be got in Brighton; and you can practise on my kiddies. It's high time Bertie and Ella learnt their A B C.'

'Patience, why are you so good to me? I—I don't deserve it.'

Suddenly her manner changes, and she becomes stern and hard.

'Patience hullingham,' she says, gazing straight before her into the fire, 'before I enter your house there is something I must tell you. If after I have told you you still desire my presence, I will come; if

28

not—well, I shouldn't blame you. I have been in the—the workhouse! There, it's out now. Take me or not, as you will;' and Mora shudders.

'Are you *mad*? You, Lady Hullingham, in the *workhouse*? I can't believe it. You are joking.'

'Do I look like it? No; it's true.'

'But when—how?'

'I was in Kensington Workhouse for five months. I have only just come out. My friends, the Heywoods, rescued me, and brought me here. I was ill, and, in the absence from town of Sir Carlos Hullingham, the officials asked me who to send to, and I gave Mrs. Heywood's address.'

'Then, Sir Carlos knew?'

'Yes, he knew. It was he who——'

'No, Mora, no! Not that!'

'Yes; Carlos placed me there under a *pseudonym*, in order to force me to return to him.'

'Return? With that woman there?'

'Yes. But until Reine Donati leaves my home I will never return— I'd die rather!'

'And you are right. Oh, my God, what a devil! How could you ever have loved such a man, Mora?'

'Others have asked that too; I sometimes ask it of myself now. Ah, Patience! if one could glance into the future, many lives might be different to what they are; but it is veiled—mercifully so, perhaps.'

'Perhaps indeed! Well, it's time, I reckon, my dear, you had a little happiness; so run away, and pack your bibs and tuckers,[5] and come along home with me. We can catch the 6.10 train, I think, if we are sharp. Good gracious, child! are you ill?'

---

[5] Bib and tucker: clothes.

29

Lady Hullingham sways suddenly forwards as the room whirls round her. Kindness has overcome her, and she faints.

*   *   *   *   *

'Where am I? Lucy! Patience! Oh, how strange!' as she recognises her friend, Miss Heywood, and Patience Hullingham bending over her.

'Yes, we're here,' says Patience briskly, giving her some water to drink. 'There, that's a trifle better'—as Mora struggles up. 'Miss Heywood has packed your box, so as soon as we've had the cup of tea she has ordered we'll be off to the train. No more troubles for you, my lady, if I can help it. Sir Carlos may flay me, but he'll not get inside Ivy Cottage to worry you.'

'Patience, you are too good to me, dear; how shall I ever repay you?'

'By getting strong and well, my dear, and helping me with the kiddies.'

'Lucy,' says Mora, tying on her bonnet at the glass above the mantelpiece, 'do you know who this is?—this woman who is heaping kindness thus upon me? She is Reville's widow! You know her story; and she does all this for me, after my husband's behaviour.'

Miss Heywood bends and kisses Mrs. Hullingham, and the tears are in her eyes.

'God bless you for your goodness to my friend!' she says.

'You look as though a blow by the sea wouldn't do *you* any harm, my young lady.[6] Run round to your mother's and fetch a nightgown and a toothbrush, and come with us for a week.'

'Patience! Do you mean it? Oh, how lovely!' cries Mora. 'Run, Lucy; your mother will be sure to let you come.'

---

[6] Blow: the act of blowing off steam, taking a break to relax.

That night Mora and her friend are at Rottingdean inhaling the brisk sea-breezes, and listening to the surge of the waves on the shore, and watching the moonlight quivering upon the waters.

'Can you believe it, Lucy, that we are here with Reville's wife? What would Carlos say? What fun—oh, what fun!' And for very gladness of heart Mora laughs aloud.

'Who cares?' says Miss Heywood derisively.

CHAPTER V
A RETROSPECT

I N order to understand the story thoroughly, and the exquisite cruelty of the man Hullingham, it becomes necessary to transport the reader back to a period of eight years ago, and present to him the death of Reville Hullingham, and the story of the blood-stained piano at Hullingham Manor.

Reville Hullingham was the second of three brothers: Carlos, himself, and Laurence, the father of the young man Frank. In general appearance, Reville closely resembled his brother Carlos, except that consumption had set its seal upon him, in the hectic flush of the hollow cheeks. His eyes were gray, and rather mournful in expression, and his chestnut beard and moustache perhaps added to the effect of delicacy. For an exact likeness of Reville Hullingham, we can refer the reader to the pictured angels of Sir E. Burne-Jones.

In the early days of their acquaintance with Mora Alderson, twenty years ago, both Carlos and Laurence loved her. Reville admired her, for she was extremely beautiful, and honoured her; and his heart ached when he saw how matters were tending between herself and his brother Carlos. By his peculiar gifts and personal fascination, Carlos quickly won the girl's affection, who, through a strange misunderstanding, believed that his wife Adelaide was the wife of his brother Reville; and not until her heart was bound up in him did she discover the truth.

Sir Carlos' first marriage was a dismal failure. He never loved his wife, and but married her to increase his fame; for she was a shining light in the world of letters, and a wealthy woman; thus, he knew that if he married her her wealth would bring him what in ability he lacked, and pave the way to fame. And Adelaide Milroy, dazzled by his glittering personality and eloquent tongue, allowed herself to love him, married him, and sealed her doom.

All went fairly well till their meeting with Miss Alderson at the house of some mutual friends, when Sir Carlos fell madly in love with the beautiful Mora. To give him his due, as soon as he found out that Miss Alderson was not indifferent to him, he coined an excuse to leave her presence; but meeting her again, some months subsequently, he lacked the moral courage to stop away.

Mora herself, poor child! was but sixteen years of age when they first met, and her fresh young beauty captured him beyond resistance, and learning that he was unhappy, she loved him all the more. No one was by to warn her that ruin must surely follow if she listened to his passionate pleadings, for her mother was dead, and her father, a military man, was busy with his regiment, and entrusted his only daughter to the questionable care of a maiden sister of his own—an aunt who loved her, for she was a winsome lassie, and allowed her all the freedom she desired. So day by day, hour by hour, she drifted nearer to the precipice, until the day came in which she sold her soul for the man she loved.

Although no word of warning came to Mora, Reville Hullingham, seeing how things must end, took upon himself to speak to his brother on the girl's behalf.

'Carlos,' he said, 'it's a cruel shame that you should seek to lead that child to ruin. So far she is innocent and pure: why blast her life, as you most surely will if you go on as you are going now?'

And Sir Carlos answered coldly, looking his brother up and down:

'Reville, my business is my own; kindly see that in future yours does not cross the paths of Miss Alderson's or mine.' And he turned to the organ, at which instrument he was an adept; for he was gifted with the soul of music, and hour after hour he would play either on the piano or on the magnificent hydraulic organ in the hall. A thrill as of some unearthly power ran through his music, which held his hearers as by a spell. It was their love of music which first formed the bond of union between himself and Mora; and many was the hour they would spend in after-years together at the organ, when as a guest she stayed at Hullingham Manor.

The years went on, and with the steady growth of Carlos' love for Mora the coldness increased between the brothers, until the day when, in consequence of Reville's marriage, the fatal quarrel came in which he died.

For years he had suffered from that most painful phase of consumption, tuberculosis, together with a weakness of the heart, and, warned that excitement or any exertion might prove fatal, lived from year to year with the sword of Damocles above his head.[7]

While spending a month by the Norfolk Broads he met with a fair young girl named Patience Conway, a farmer's daughter, the only child at the farm whereat he lodged. Many hours they passed together beside the Broads, or beneath the trees in her father's garden, till, although of lower rank, her purity and simple truth captivated him, and, with her parents' consent, he married her one day in the little village church.

Bringing his bride to London, he went one day to Hullingham Manor, and broke the news of his marriage to his brother Carlos.

---

[7] Damocles was forced by King Dionysius II to sit beneath a razor-sharp sword, suspended above his head by a single strand of horsehair, to demonstrate the impossibility of enjoying the fruits of life, of being happy, whilst labouring under the spectre of death.

At this time Adelaide was dead, and Mora Alderson had become Lady Hullingham.

It must be mentioned here that, by a clause in their father's will, Sir Carlos Hullingham was made sole arbiter of his brothers' fortunes. Generous to a fault, he apportioned off a handsome allowance alike to Reville and Laurence.

But when he learnt that Reville had made a *mésalliance*,[8] his anger knew no bounds, and insolently he ordered him from the house, telling him that he had disgraced his father's name, and that from that hour he might look elsewhere for the wherewithal to live, but that not one farthing of Hullingham money should go to maintain a low-bred hussy from a farm.

'You have cast in your lot with the *canaille* of the earth;[9] you may look to them for subsistence from to-day. Never again shall you darken the doors of Hullingham Manor, and never again, with my consent, shall the name of Reville Hullingham be mentioned within these walls. You are no longer my brother; I disown you. Go!' and, ringing the bell, to the old butler who answered it, he said: 'Rowlands, show this gentleman out; he has disgraced his family and name. Under no pretext whatsoever is he to be admitted to my house. He is no more a brother of mine.'

'Sir Carlos! Master Reville!' the old servant cried in great distress. He had served their family for thirty years.

'No words, Rowlands, but obey me,' said Sir Carlos coldly.

Without a word Reville Hullingham left the room, his face white, his heart crushed with pain.

As he passed into the hall, Lady Hullingham rose and swiftly

---

[8] An unsuitable marriage.

[9] *Canaille*: riffraff, rabble, the common masses.

followed him. Angrily her husband called her back, but she turned and faced him by the door.

'In most things I am ready to obey you, Carlos; in others *I* am the mistress of my actions, and this is one,' she said, with a quiet dignity that cowed him. 'You have openly insulted and disowned your brother Reville; I have not.' And she passed into the hall, closing the door behind her.

'Send me your address, Reville,' she said unsteadily; 'for while I live you and your wife shall never lack a friend. I am more pained than I can say at Carlos' behaviour; I consider he has treated you infamously; but, believe me, Reville, I am not, and never shall be, a party to it. Good-bye, dear, and may every blessing be yours in your married life!'

'Bless you, little sister!' Reville said. 'Carlos will be sorry for this some day. Good-bye, good-bye, Mora!'

Heavy at heart, Lady Hullingham watched his retreating figure till he was out of sight, then sadly closed the door and returned to the drawing-room.

She never saw her brother-in-law again alive.

The months passed by and turned to years, and, unknown to Sir Carlos, Mora sent the bulk of her allowance to Reville and his wife at their little cottage at Rottingdean, near Brighton.

At last Reville's health broke down, and as a last resource he was ordered to Madeira. At great cost to her pride, his wife, Patience Hullingham, made this verdict known to Sir Carlos. Her letter he tore in half and returned in an envelope unread.

But growing alarmingly worse, Reville himself determined to force his brother to an interview, and wrest from him the means to reach Madeira.

With this end in view, he went to Hullingham Manor, and,

watching his opportunity, entered by the drawing-room window, and confronted his brother alone.

Speechless with anger, yet horrified at the change in his brother's appearance, for a moment Sir Carlos seemed turned to stone. But passion conquered and convulsed him.

'I believe I desired you never to set foot in this house again, Mr. Reville Hullingham. How is it that you are here, sneaking in through the windows like a thief?'

'Look at me and see!' said Reville sadly. 'If I had rung the hand-door bell, your servants would have driven me away. Carlos, I am a dying man; can you deny me the only chance whereby to live?'

'You have no claim upon my bounty. Must I ring for the servants to show you out, or will you go by the way you came, unseen?'

With the merciless cruelty of his nature, he stood and smiled. But a change came over Reville, and he seemed endowed with a new weird strength, the strange strength given to the dying; and, standing by the grand pianoforte in the window, he turned and faced his brother, his eyes filled with ineffable contempt.

'No!' he said. 'I'll stay, Sir Carlos Hullingham. I will stay until you hand to me that portion that is my due. I have a wife and little children; why should I die and leave them to starve, when, as I am told, in a warmer climate I may live?'

'Highly melodramatic, but totally without effect upon me,' said Sir Carlos heartlessly. 'You have chosen your path: walk in it. Not one sixpence of Hullingham money will you get from me. Now go.'

'Carlos! Have you no heart, no pity? I am your brother, Carlos; can you turn me—a dying man—from your door, when fifty pounds, a trifle to you, might save my life?'

'Come, I've had enough of this, Reville Hullingham. As you have lived in the past, so you can live in the future. Go!' and he pointed to the open window.

'If I go, Carlos Hullingham, God's curse will rest upon you, my murderer; for——'

A spasm of pain crossed his wan features, and a fit of coughing stopped his speech.

'For if I go, I must surely die. Think! before it is too late.'

The words which would have moved another man to pity had but the effect of rousing Hullingham's passion; and with an oath he sprang forward, and seized his brother by the throat, forcing him backwards towards the window.

A sharp cry rang through the room, and Reville staggered, and fell across the open pianoforte, a thin stream of blood trickling through his lips. A sigh and one convulsive shiver, and he was dead!

Livid with fear, Sir Carlos stared at him, transfixed with horror; then, softly approaching, touched and called him.

'Reville! Reville! In mercy, speak! He's dead! Oh, God! oh, God! what have I done, what have I doe?'

The slowly increasing pool of blood was the only answer, dyeing the framework of the pianoforte with a crimson stain between the strings, the record of a tale that no time can efface.

Sir Carlos rang the bell, and explained to the frightened butler and to his wife, who entered simultaneously, that his brother's death was due to the fracture of a blood vessel in the lungs, in the course of a stolen interview.

Lady Hullingham bent upon him a searching gaze, and he saw by the expression in her eyes that she had read the truth.

''Leave him to me,' she said. 'Your touch would be an insult: his death lies at your door.'

A thousand demon voices seemed to fill the room with derisive laughter, while the words rang in his ears: 'If I go, God's curse will rest upon you, my murderer!' and Sir Carlos went away, half mad with fear.

With Rowlands' help and with many bitter tears, Mora laid the poor thin body upon the couch, and with her handkerchief wiped the blood-stains from the hollow cheeks, and closed his eyes.

'Reville!' she cried; 'poor, poor, dear Reville! You have found the joy which in life, through Carlos, was denied you. Rest in peace.'

She went to the conservatory, and, gathering an armful of chrysanthemums, laid them upon his breast.

And the news of her husband's death was gently broken to his widow, in a letter from Lady Hullingham, that day.

CHAPTER VI
WARP AND WOOF IN THE LOOM OF FATE

T O return to the present.

It is late next morning when Mora awakes to find Miss Heywood up and dressed, arranging a tasty little breakfast, which Mrs. Hullingham has sent up to her, upon a small table by her bedside.

'Lucy dear, how lovely! I didn't expect this. What a darling Patience is! But how we have wronged her all these years!'

'Mrs. Hullingham is a true Christian, Mora. It isn't many women who, after the treatment of Sir Carlos, would act like this to his wife. What a pretty little place this is! I've been out already; the sea is lovely. I've been to the church too—such a dear little old-fashioned church!—and the children showed me their father's grave. Poor fellow! I couldn't help shuddering when I thought of his terrible fate.'

Later in the day Mrs. Hullingham informs her guests that she has need to go into Brighton for some shopping, and invites their company. Lucy goes, but Mora, pleading fatigue, prefers to remain with the children at home.

Soon after they have started, she takes her hat and coat, and accompanied by Bertie, a little man of four, goes out for a walk by the sea. The child begins a search for crabs and seaweed, as the tide is low, and Lady Hullingham is left to her own thoughts.

Walking slowly, up and down, along the shore, she presently becomes aware that a man, who likewise is strolling to and fro, is earnestly surveying her, with what seems to her as somewhat impertinent scrutiny. She turns away in hesitation, for it seems to her that the man's face is in some way familiar, yet she cannot remember having met him before. Still, she knows the features well: the overhanging brows and the shaggy hair, the shifty eyes with their bristling lashes, the mouth with the fringe of red stubbly beard. The horror of the face, the evil light in the eyes, she knows them well; but where has she seen them before? Her brain is dazed with recent trouble, and her memory fails.

Presently the man approaches her, and, raising his hat, addresses her.

'Pardon me, but I fancy we have met before?' he says, courteously enough.

Mora looks at him uneasily. What business has he to speak to her? she thinks angrily. Oh, if she could get away! But politeness requires that he shall answer him, and she say coldly:

'Possibly. I seem to know your face, but I cannot remember having met you, or your name.'

'My name is Richard Braiser,' he says with a leer. 'I had the pleasure of meeting you, madam, on the occasion of the death of a patient of mine, the late Lady Hullingham, who was for some years an inmate of my asylum.'

Mora recoils, as from some noxious reptile: all is plain to her now.

'I remember,' she says frigidly. 'I am obliged to you, sir, for acknowledging your identity; but I must beg you to excuse me. As a friend of the late Adelaide Hullingham's, I cannot entertain an acquaintanceship with Dr. Richard Braiser. Maybe he will understand, when I tell him that I am Sir Carlos Hullingham's second wife, and that he has no secrets from me!' and coldly she moves away, calling her little nephew.

As though thunderstruck, the doctor gazes after her, a sickly pallor overspreading his evil countenance, and through clenched teeth he hisses, picking at his lips:

'His *wife*, is she? Well, I never thought he'd marry her. Curse her! I'll be even with her yet!'

Will he? We shall see.

Passing through the village, Lady Hullingham and her small companion ascend the hill to the quaint old church, and Mora, remembering her brother-in-law's grave, bids the child lead her to it.

'Me puts f'owers on it evewy day, Aunt Morwa,' the little fellow says, looking up into her face proudly, as they enter the churchyard gate, 'An' mine lasts longer than mover's, too. She says it's 'cos I'se a little child. Is it, Aunt Morwa?'

Lady Hullingham smiles sadly as she looks down at the little fatherless boy.

'Very likely, darling. God loves little children, and probably He keeps your flowers fresh in order to show you He loves you.'

'Iss,' says Berrie sagely. Then, in another tone: 'Aunt Morwa! There's sich a bootifu' g'ave over there, with a big w'ite c'oss on it; an' evewy day a lady comes an' looks at it an' puts some f'owers on it, an' goes away kying. Mover sometimes puts some f'owers on it, too, an' so does I, but I don't know who's the lady in the g'ave, Aunt Morwa. Mover says she's a bootifu' lady who was vewy unhappy, an' she's a saint in heaven now!'

Such a long speech for such a little man, delivered breathlessly, and with many a gasp!

'A lady who was unhappy, Bertie?' says Mora, with sudden faintness. 'Where is the grave? Show me, dear!'

'Dare 'tis, Aunt Morwa—over dare, by the big t'ees.'

SACRED

TO THE MEMORY

OF

ADELAIDE MILROY HULLINGHAM

Only too well she knew what the name would be, yet the sight of it is more than she can bear. She throws her arms around the cross, and sobs as if her heart would break.

'Adelaide, Adelaide, forgive me! Oh, God, forgive me! Have I not suffered enough to make atonement? Forgive us—Carlos and me—for the grievous wrong we did this woman who is dead;' and, weeping, she lays her head against the cold marble of the cross.

Awestruck, little Bertie creeps up to her, tears of sympathy in his baby eyes, and slips his tiny fingers into hers.

'Don't ky, Aunt Morwa!' he says piteously, his lips quivering. 'What for oo ky? Did oo love the lady too?'

'Yes, yes, Bertie dear,' poor Mora sobs. 'I loved her too—so much, oh, so much! Bertie'—and she recovers herself with difficulty, and draws the child close to her, kneeling by the grave—'she was your own dear Auntie Adelaide, who—who died long ago.'

'Poor Auntie Adelaide!'

To the lot of few of us, mercifully, does it fall to stand by the grave of one whom we have deeply wronged, or been even the indirect cause of another's wronging. Mora, standing by Adelaide Hullingham's last resting-place, feels that a whole life of torment would scarcely atone for one day in the years of agony the dead woman had undergone, and words, prayers, fail to convey the sense of hopeless remorse for what is past recall.

And looking upon the evidence of her husband's hypocrisy, she shudders. Oh, the mockery of that handsome tomb! erected but to pander to Hullingham's mania for ambition, for which he has wrecked his happiness and home, and sacrificed those hapless members of his family who chanced to stand in his way. The beautiful sculptured cross, overspread with the rank moss of years— the little dust-begrimed aucuba bushes, and the untrimmed grass, dead leaves, and other refuse, bespeaking the lack of care—placed in the most conspicuous place in the churchyard, where the eyes of all comers must perforce rest upon it, and read that here lies the beloved wife of Carlos Hullingham.

'Liar! Ye gods, ye gods, the mockery!' cries Mora, and, sick at heart, she turns away and moves across to Reville's grave, led thither by his little son.

Presently, through the churchyard gate, there comes a woman, attired in the black uniform of a hospital nurse. She walks direct to Adelaide Hullingham's tomb, upon which she places a wreath of passion-flowers, white and blue. For several moments she kneels by the grave, seemingly in prayer; then with a sigh she rises, and turning to go, reveals the tear-stained face of Sister Janet Stirling, the asylum nurse.

Glancing at Mora as she passes down the path, she starts, and Mora, as she recognises the woman who had sent her the confession, and whom last she saw by Adelaide' death-bed, draws back with a low cry.

'So, Lady Hullingham!' the nurse says sternly. 'I knew this day would come, though I scarcely thought so soon. Has my prediction been fulfilled?'

'To the full, Nurse Stirling. My husband deserted me.'

Sister Janet breaks into a harsh laugh.

'I knew he would! That, I suppose, is the least he has done?' And she laughs again.

'You are right,' says Mora coldly; 'but I think your laughter slightly out of place. I have sinned, it is true, and I have wronged the dead, yet, if you knew the suffering I have borne at the hands of Sir Carlos Hullingham, I think that even you would pity me, and consider I have atoned.'

'No suffering which you could ever endure, Mora Alderson, could in any way atone for the murder of Adelaide Hullingham, of which murder I hold *you* guilty.'

'Me?' Mora starts back, and her face grows pale.

'In my eyes,' the nurse goes on mercilessly; 'her death lies at your door, and yours alone. But for you, the man Carlos Hullingham, in himself but a weak profligate, would never have imagined the inhuman tortures he inflicted upon that wretched woman. Indifference does not spur the heart to murder: hatred does. Up to the time when you crossed his path, he was but indifferent to his wife; but, fired by his unholy passion for *you*, he planned her martyrdom and the fraud which led to her death. From first to last he was but a tool in the hand of a fiend roused within him by you; and *you*, and *you alone*, I hold to be Adelaide Hullingham's murderess.'

'Stay, Nurse Stirling. By the high heaven above us, you wrong me!' Mora cries, her eyes dilating with horror at the other's words. 'I knew nothing of Adelaide's martyrdom until from her confession I learnt it. I knew only what Sir Carlos told me, that she was mad; and during her years of suffering at Hullingham Manor, prior to her madness, I was led to believe, both by herself and him, that through illness she was obliged to keep to her room. Ah, no, Nurse Stirling! I loved Adelaide too dearly ever to wish her harm; and, strange to say, although I loved her husband as intensely as I did, I never felt one pang of jealousy for his wife, or realized the wrong I did her by that love.'

'The greatest wrong one woman can offer to another,' the nurse says cruelly.

'Yes; I know it now, Nurse Stirling; but then I was young—I was ignorant; and the sin was hidden by the glamour of the love I bore to Carlos.'

'Ah! Well, there's something in that, it is true. Perhaps I've been a little hard upon you, Lady Hullingham,' she says, relenting, and holding out her hand.

'You have, Nurse Stirling,' says Mora gently; 'but I thank you for admitting it.' Then, after a pause: 'You may not believe me, Nurse Stirling; but, unlike Adelaide, my love for Sir Carlos Hullingham has turned to the most bitter hatred and contempt.'

Her eyes glow with a lurid flame, and an expression so deadly comes into her face that the nurse is fairly startled. She had not deemed her capable of the force of passion that speaks in every feature and flashes in her eyes.

'I have determined,' she goes on, 'that before the year is out he shall be punished as he deserves, both he and his accomplice, Richard Braiser.'

'Is this indeed the truth?' asks Sister Janet, with a grim smile. 'If it is, Lady Hullingham, I am prepared to bury the hatchet, and for Adelaide's sake to help you to fulfil your design; for no earthly punishment can be too hard for criminals such as they. How do you propose to act?'

'I intend to make public Adelaide's confession.'

Even Nurse Stirling shudders, and grows pale.

'What a dreadful retribution!' she whispers.

'That is not all,' says Lady Hullingham, staring with unseeing eyes over the little village clustered at their feet, and across to the even square of ocean, which, mirror-like, extends to the horizon, broken but by a stray fishing-smack or a passing steamer. 'That is not all,' she repeats stonily; 'I intend also to reveal the details of his brother Reville's death, with whose widow I am staying here. That is her little boy over there by the church porch. She lives at Ivy Cottage; will you come and see me there to-morrow, and I will introduce you to Mrs. Hullingham, when we can talk this matter over at our leisure?'

'Very well, I'll come.'

'How is it you are here, Nurse Stirling?' asks Mora as they are parting at the gate. 'Surely you are not at that asylum still?'

'Don't mention the name! No, I left the day after Adelaide died, but I live here in order to be near the grave of the woman who was dearer to me than the dearest sister. I am in private nursing now—is only three miles from here, and the man Braiser hovers about like a bird of evil omen. He fears me, for he knows I am in possession of his guilty secret. One day I may be called upon to speak, and then, God grant, he will receive his due.'

'That time is nearer than you think, Nurse Stirling. On New Year's Eve, at midnight, the blow must fall; but how is the matter I have to decide. Perhaps you can help me. Though my love for Carlos Hullingham is dead, I prefer that he should suffer for his crimes on earth, rather than in an eternity of condemnation.'

CHAPTER VII
CONSPIRATORS

'IS it not too dramatic?'

'I think not. It is necessary to be as convincing as possible, or it may fail in its effect upon Carlos, and I am sure it would upon Braiser.'

'Wicked as they are, I feel almost sorry for them. What a terrible awakening!'

The speakers, Patience, Mora, and Nurse Stirling, with Lucy Heywood, are sitting round the tea-table in Mrs. Hullingham's cosy drawing-room at Ivy Cottage.

'It will be easy enough to get the Recital introduced into Lady Mountjoy's soirée,' says Nurse Stirling. 'She is an old friend of mine, and will do anything I ask of her, in reason. I will enlist her sympathies in our cause under the belief that she is assisting an aspiring artiste; and, if I know her, she will grab at so weird a novelty as a Phantom Recital! The only hitch that I can see is the lateness of the hour. You say, Lady Hullingham, that it is absolutely requisite that the Recital should take place at midnight?'

'Absolutely. There is a record in the annals of the Hullinghams, that, when retributive justice falls upon a member of their house, it is at the stroke of midnight, on New Year's Eve, that the blow falls. Carlos, like all Spaniards, is intensely superstitious, and, knowing nothing of the confession, will imagine the Recital, as I shall do it, a voice from the dead. Then will come the retribution, which will be the public unveiling of his character before the world, which till now he has blinded, and then the judgment.'

'The judgment?' queries Mrs. Hullingham.

'The punishment of both himself and Braiser shall rest upon the verdict pronounced upon them by Lady Mountjoy's assembled guests; who, I take it, will be all of them men and women of honour and impartiality. If they vote for legal punishment, the confession, as it stands, shall be delivered next day to the police at Scotland Yard, by Nurse Stirling, and she and I will give whatever evidence is required. Mine, as Lady Hullingham, will be worthless, except as in corroboration.'

'Mora dear, you are very merciless. Remember, Sir Carlos is your husband, after all.' says Lucy Heywood.

'Circumstances have combined to make me merciless. Sir Carlos is to me now but a dastardly criminal, besides being a coward and a cur; and I cannot rest until he is punished as he deserves, whatever I may feel afterwards—if there is an afterwards,' she adds musingly.

'What do you mean?' asks Mrs. Hullingham, startled.

Mora smiles enigmatically, but meeting the eyes of Sister Janet fixed upon her, she sees that the nurse has read the truth—that her days are numbered.

'In a way, Lady Hullingham and I are criminals, too,' says Nurse Stirling quietly after a pause.

'What?' from Lucy and Patience, in one voice.

'We may be held guilty of compounding a felony, inasmuch as that we concealed our knowledge of the conspiracy. Lady Hullingham would in all probability be acquitted, because she has turned Queen's evidence, but I have only done so indirectly, as, but for her decision to expose the felony, I should have held my tongue until the end, in accordance with my promise to the dead. But of this we must take our chance, if the fraud is to be exposed at all.'

'Yes,' says Mora absently; 'we must take our chance. For myself,

I am indifferent, but I should be sorry to drag you into any trouble, Nurse Stirling.'

'Never mind me,' says the nurse abruptly. 'What I do I do with my eyes open. But now as to this soirée. How do you propose to work your programme.'

'I want a paragraph inserted, if possible, in the Society Column of the *Daily Gazette*, announcing that a novel feature in the way of recitals will be introduced at Lady Mountjoy's forthcoming *soirée musicale*. Then I want a card of invitation sent to the editor, in order that the proceedings my be publicly made known throughout England. As to the Recital, I must speak from behind a thick transparency, so that my form be dimly visible, illumined by limelight, but my identity as Lady Hullingham concealed; for I want the whole thing to be as ghostly as possible.'

'How gruesome! I should think it will about finish Braiser and my Lord Carlos,' laughs Lucy.

Mora smiles grimly.

'How did your brain devise such a horrible arrangement?' asks Mrs. Hullingham. 'I wouldn't stand in those men's shoes for something, when the confession is recited under those conditions. How did you think of it?'

'I don't know; it came to me as by an inspiration, both the Recital and the manner of reciting it—as also the costume.'

'What costume do you intend to wear for it? Greek?' asks Lucy, interested.

'Wait until the time comes, and you will see,' says Lady Hullingham. Then to Nurse Stirling: 'Will you undertake the "stage management" for me Sister Janet? As Lady Mountjoy is your friend, it is better, I think, that you should make the arrangements with her. I shall require a small platform, with curtains to draw from a centre, a stretched transparency of as thick net as possible, so as almost to veil me from sight. That can be hired from any theatrical shop at little cost. Then I shall want limelight, and that is all. Do you understand?'

'I think so,' says the nurse meditatively. I will run up to town to-morrow and call upon Lady Mountjoy, and make all clear; and if you will write the paragraph for the papers, I will see that it is put in. Then there will be the invitations. Braiser and Hullingham must both have one, and we four here. Is there anyone else?'

'If my nephew, Frank Hullingham, might be present, I should be glad,' says Mora.

'Very well. Those, with the newspaper man, will be all. I'll make a note of them, in case I forget; and then I must go, as I am due at a case.'

'I saw that man Braiser yesterday, Nurse Stirling,' says Lady Hullingham, as she accompanies the visitor to the door. 'I feel that if I were long in his vicinity I should kill him.'

'Yes,' says the other, smiling; 'men like him inspire such feelings; I sometimes feel the same myself. Good-bye.'

CHAPTER VIII
AN ADVERTISEMENT, AND TWO INVITATIONS

T WO days later all fashionable London is astir with the intelligence that the festive Lady Mountjoy is about to inaugurate a novelty at her forthcoming *soirée musicale*, advertised to take place at her own residence, in Grosvenor Gardens, on New Year's Eve, and at which everyone who is anyone will be present. It is furthermore announced that the soirée will commence at the unusually late hour of ten o'clock, in order to accommodate the requirements of the event of the evening—viz., a Phantom Recital. People are agog with excitement. Why 'phantom'? and who is the reciter? are amongst the numerous questions asked. The idea is gruesome enough to be tantalizing, and curiosity such as it inspires can be satisfied but by witnessing the Recital. Consequently all London flocks to Lady Mountjoy's 'afternoon' that day, angling for invitations.

'So energetic of you, dear Lady Mountjoy!' one says, fawning upon her hostess by the tea-table. 'You always contrive to secure for the amusement of your guests some novelties which no one else could have imagined. This Phantom Recital that we are to hear at your delightful soirée'—the speaker has not been asked—'will be a very interesting spectacle, I should imagine?'

'Yes, very interesting,' says Lady Mountjoy.

'The reciter,' says another, 'must be a clever man, I should think, to dream of such a thing?'

'Yes, very clever,' says Lady Mountjoy.

She is one of those plump little women, with a quizzical face full of fun, *piquante* features, and eyes that twinkle with suppressed amusement as she mocks at the persons who toady her, fishing for invitations which she has no intention of giving. As a leader of the highest circles of London society, her house is always thronged; for, besides being an ideal hostess, she is a kindly, genial little body with a bright word and a smile for come who may, and she openly quizzes the shams in the world around her and the hollowness of society etiquette.

In this morning's *Social Gossip* there appears a paragraph which sets men talking:

'An interesting feature, we understand, will be introduced at the *soirée musicale* at Countess Mountjoy's residence in Grosvenor Gardens on New Year's Eve. We allude to what is rather ambiguously termed a Phantom Recital. What this item in the programme will prove to be we are at present unable to say, but it is whispered on good authority that some strange revelations will be made concerning a certain personage in high life, and impatiently we await an event which we are led to believe will set many tongues a-wagging.

'That the Phantom Recital will prove a success is a foregone conclusion, seeing that it will bear the stamp of the presence of Royalty.'

By the first post to-day two invitations are received respectively by Sir Carlos Hullingham and Dr. Richard Braiser.

Invitation I:

'Countess Mountjoy at home Thursday evening, the 31st int. *Soirée musicale*, 10p.m. to 4 a.m. R.S.V.P.'

And on the top, in her ladyship's bold calligraphy: 'Sir Carlos Hullingham.' The card, enclosed in a scented envelope bearing the Mountjoy coronet and crest, is laid upon the breakfast-table with other letters at Hullingham Manor.

'H'm!' mutters Carlos as he reads it. 'I must go, I suppose; she'll be offended if I don't put in an appearance. What's this?—the 31st? By Heaven, that's New Year's Eve! Ah—h—h! I can breathe again! What luck! So much for Mora's threat now!'—snapping his fingers. 'Ha, ha, ha!' he laughs airily. 'On New Year's Eve, at midnight, I shall be at Grosvenor Gardens. I'm free—free from that burdening fear, thank the gods—oh, thank the gods! Yet it is strange, that vision of my brother's spirit and Mora's letter. It was too real to be a dream. The letter is substantial enough'—taking it from his pocket and reading it again for the hundredth time. ' "At midnight the blow shall fall." Midnight! Let me see'—referring to the card again— ' "10 p.m. to 4 a.m." What an ungodly hour! But it includes the hour of midnight. That for you, my Lady Mora!' and he blows over the tips of his fingers.

At about this time a similar coroneted envelope (Invitation 2) is handed to Dr. Braiser, at Braiser's Asylum for the Insane, at ——. Opening it, a card drops out—an invitation to a soirée at a stranger's house. He glances at it curiously, and proceeds to read the covering letter, which runs as follows:

'100, Grosvenor Gardens, S. W.

'Countess Mountjoy presents her compliments to Dr. Richard Braiser.

'Having heard from Sir Carlos Hullingham, of Hullingham Manor, ——, that he is a clever brain specialist, and also that he possesses a small private asylum for persons of unsound mind, she

54

writes to beg his presence at her house for an examination of a niece of her own, in whom she fears incipient insanity. Lady Mountjoy will be glad if Dr. Braiser will make it convenient to call upon her at the above address.

'As she deems it essential that the patient should be in ignorance of the reason for the doctor's presence, Lady Mountjoy begs to enclose a card for a soirée she is giving on the 31st inst., at which her niece will be among the guests, and at which Dr. Braiser will be able to contemplate her case at leisure. Lady Mountjoy begs that Dr. Braiser will let nothing stand in the way of his presence at the soirée, or allow money to be a consideration.'

'Whew! This may mean a pot o' cash, Dick, my boy! The 31st, eh? H'm! let me see. That's New Year's Eve, ain't it? A free time for me, too. Yes, I'll run up to town that day, put up at Grosvenor that night, and return here the following day. What a spree! Good biz, too—deuced good biz! Mountjoy! That's a big name. Swell. By Jove! may book a patient, and pave the way for more amongst the upper ten. A few o' that sort would suit me nicely. First-class London connection, eh? Dick, my boy, you're in luck, and this through Hullingham, too! Good man not to forget poor old Dick! Hope I'll see him at the show. Wonder what's brought his wife to Rottingdean? Awkward her knowing that little affair of my lady Adelaide. What a confounded ass he was to tell her! Deuced unpleasant for both of us if anything of that got out! I'm always on hot bricks as to what that d——d nurse may do. How do I know she'll hold her tongue for ever?'

So do the meshes of Destiny's web entangle the feet of these men to draw them to their doom.

CHAPTER IX
NEW YEAR'S EVE

A T Lady Mountjoy's house in Grosvenor Gardens all is bustle and confusion. Workmen and servants rush hither and thither, arranging and rearranging the furniture, hanging curtains and Chinese lanterns in various nooks and corners of the great double drawing-rooms and spacious, palm-decked conservatory. From a florist's cart at the door waving palms and exotic flowers are brought in to fill up recesses and form a floral screen for the Hungarian band. Carpenters are busy upon the erection of the awning from the door to the street, and upon a small platform across a corner of the larger drawing-room.

A hansom stops at the house, and Nurse Stirling descends, pays the man, and enters through the open door. She passes unannounced through the hall to a small apartment at the farther end, which is used as a boudoir by her ladyship. Miss Stirling knocks an enters.

'Is that you, Janet? I am so glad you have come,' says Lady Mountjoy, who, swathed in a big holland apron, is arranging flowers in various vases and épergnes upon a low Pembroke table.[10] Miss Stirling bends and kisses her.

'You are very busy, Bertha. Can I help?'

'Yes, my dear, you can, but not with these. I am at my wits' end

---

[10] Épergne: a table centrepiece, usually made of silver, that sits on four or five feet and supports a central bowl, from which four or more smaller bowls are held by radiating branches. It can be used to hold food, flowers, candles or ornamental objects.

about your platform, in case they do it wrong You had better go and see to it yourself. I suppose Mademoiselle Mora has given you full instructions as to what she wants? These professionals are so exacting.'

'I believe that as a rule they are; but you will not find Mademoiselle Mora exacting. She is a quiet woman, and easily pleased. I have a list of her few requirements.'

'I never asked her fee; do you know it, Janet?'

'Nothing to-night. It is her début, you remember. She is so grateful to you for allowing her to give her Recital at your house, that she prefers to take no fee.'

'By what you tell me, she seems a pleasant person,' says Lady Mountjoy.

'She is a fascinating little woman, and once was very beautiful, but worry and trouble have gone a good way to spoil her looks. Poor thing! her days in this world are numbered; she won't live long.'

'How very sad!' says Lady Mountjoy. 'What is the cause of her illness?'

'Rapid decline; and she is much worse than she herself believes.'

'Poor girl!' cries her ladyship again. 'What brought it on?'

'A life of bitter suffering at the hands of a husband who is a devil!'

'Husband! She is married, then?'

'Yes; she is married. Mademoiselle Mora is her professional name.'

'I shall take a deeper interest in her Recital now you have told me this. I hope it will be a success.'

'The Recital will be of greater interest to you, and to your guests, than you dream of, Bertha!'

'But, Janet——'

'You promised to ask no questions, didn't you, Bertha?' says Nurse Stirling, smiling. 'I told you that the Recital was designed in order to make public a grievous wrong, which for too long has lain undiscovered. More at present I must not tell you.'

'Well, I must be patient, I suppose. But you make me curious, I must admit.'

Miss Stirling smiles.

'Don't forget to lock the doors to-night, Bertha, when the lights go down.'

'I won't forget, though I don't understand why you want them locked.'

'Because the criminals will both be present at the soirée!'

'Janet! My dear girl, you make me nervous; really, I must insist on knowing more. Remember I have my guests to consider.'

'I perfectly understand,' says Miss Stirling gravely. 'Your guests one and all will greatly thank you for what will be revealed to-night, for there is a devil in your midst, from whose face the veil will be removed.'

'Is Dr. Braiser connected with this mystery in any way?' asks Lady Mountjoy.

'Yes, but he is not the man I mean; he is but the tool in the hands of a greater monster—a fiend in the guise of man!'

'But'—and Lady Mountjoy hesitates—'but Dr. Braiser is the only man who will be here to-night that is a stranger to me. Everyone else is of our "set." Janet, what can you mean?' And the poor lady begins to grow alarmed.

'The person to whom I refer,' Nurse Stirling goes on steadily, without removing her eyes from Lady Mountjoy's face, 'is almost the leader of your "set"; and more, he is a close friend both of your own and of Lord Mountjoy's, Bertha. Now, not a word more! Time will show you all; I'm going to see to the platform!' And, laughing, Nurse Stirling runs away.

*　　　*　　　*　　　*　　　*

It is half-past ten. The reception-rooms at Grosvenor Gardens are ablaze with light, and brilliant with jewels and flowers, and the showy dresses of women in the latest miracles of fashion. The buzz of conversation ebbs and flows, and Lady Mountjoy, in a tasteful gown of myrtle green, bustles to and fro, a busy bee in her social hive.

All eyes are impatiently turned to the clocks, and towards a crimson-plush-curtained platform, before which are grouped flowers and ferns in artistic profusion.

A servant enters, and, approaching his mistress, whispers a word in her ear. She bows her head, and contrives to slip unnoticed from the room.

In her boudoir below she discovers a stranger.

It is Dr. Braiser!

Greeting him courteously, yet not without some inward shrinking, as her eyes rest upon his evil face, Lady Mountjoy thanks him for his presence.

'A person capable of any crime!' is her unspoken thought.

'May I ask how I might identify my patient?' asks the doctor suddenly.

'My niece, Miss Gabrielle Rayburn, will be dressed in pink, with diamonds in her hair. You will easily pick her out,' says her ladyship, repressing a smile; then she leads him to the drawing-rooms, where the strains of the Hungarian band fill the air with music above the hum of conversation and the trill of women's laughter.

Lady Mountjoy beckons to a gentleman standing by, and after a word with him aside she introduces the doctor to him, and bids him see that the stranger is made to feel at home; and the two men walk off together through the crowd.

'What is that platform for?' inquires Braiser shortly, when they are standing near it.

His companion, Lord Dartmoor, raises his brows in surprise.

'You have not heard of the event of the evening, the Phantom Recital, of which all London has been talking? I'm surprised!'

'I must plead absence from town as my excuse,' says Braiser, smiling. 'I live in a little out-of-the-way Sussex town where we get but little news of the busy world.'

'Ah!' say Lord Dartmoor, and they turn to other topics.

'Which is Miss Gabrielle Rayburn among the ladies here?' asks Braiser presently. 'Her ladyship pointed her out to me, but I failed to notice her among the crowd. We were speaking of her downstairs.'

'What the———' But his thought stops there. 'That is she, over by the band,' says he aloud, 'speaking to that tall military man, Colonel Bonchurch—the girl in pink, with the diamonds in her hair.'

'Oh!' says the doctor incredulously. 'Pardon me, my lord, but are you not mistaken?'

Lord Dartmoor laughs heartily.

'Who should know Gabrielle Rayburn if not I, seeing she will be my wife within a month?' he says.

The effect of his words on Braiser is electrical.

'Your—your *wife*, did you say, my lord?' he gasps. 'Surely you will not *marry* her—at least, at present?' He looks from the soldierly young fellow at his side to the opposite side of the room, with growing confusion, if not with consternation, for in the fair face of Miss Gabrielle Rayburn, laughing merrily at some quaint saying of the old Colonel's, there is no trace of madness.

'What the deuce is the matter with this chap?' thinks Lord Dartmoor, as he glances askance at the doctor at his side. 'Is he mad? What does he mean by his insolence? Low cast of countenance. How the dickens did he get here?' And as soon as he can, without rudeness, he moves away from his uncouth companion.

Other arrivals and songs and music fill up the time till past eleven; yet still the red plush curtains remain closed. It is too tantalizing!

'Sir Carlos Hullingham!' announces a servant from the doorway, in stentorian tones.

The pampered favourite enters, to be greeted with murmurs of pleasurable admiration.

'Hullo!' thinks Braiser, scrutinizing the Baronet as he advances down the room. 'Looks thin and worried. Handsome as ever! Devilish good-looking fellow, but as bad as they make 'em!'

Gliding among the throng, for Hullingham's graceful walk can be described by no other word, with his slow side smile, as he bows to one and another on his way, he comes upon Braiser leaning against a pedestal beneath a giant palm, and stops dead short. A spasmodic, indrawn breath, and his countenance changes to an ashen pallor.

'Braiser! What——'

The words die on his lips, but it is enough. The doctor sees only too plainly that a mystery is brewing, for Hullingham's face is convulsed with fear.

The clocks strike the half-hour—half-past eleven; and almost simultaneously an electric bell is rung upon the platform, and the lights are lowered to a mysterious gloom as the band commences a weird melody. Excitement runs riot through the assembly, and every voice is hushed to silence, broken but by muffled exclamations of anticipation.

Unknown to the guests, both doors are locked, and the keys in the pocket of her ladyship, who stations herself by the entrance archway.

A silence of death pervades the rooms as the plush curtains are withdrawn, in heavy folds of luminous and sombre red.

An 'act drop' is revealed, upon which is painted, true to life, a beautiful garden, the gray gables of a house between the trees, and, beyond, the sea.

'Good God!' cries Braiser in a stifled voice to Hullingham, 'it is the asylum grounds! What does it mean? Man, why are we here?'

'Stay by me,' says Hullingham with an uneasy laugh, yet clutching at the doctor's arm. 'It is uncanny, certainly, but it may be but coincidence.'

Strange that these two men should be standing side by side, drawn together by the magnetism of crime!'

Pr-r-r-ng! goes the electric bell once more, and the 'drop' is raised, to discover a sparsely-furnished room—a plain deal table, a chair, some books, and pens and ink and paper upon the table, at which there is a woman reading. She is a hospital nurse, attired in her nurse's garb. It is Sister Janet Stirling.

The scene is misty and scarcely visible, through what appears to be a moving, ever-rising vapour.

The music dies away to silence, and presently the nurse rises, and, without a word, walks off the stage. Around the audience all is dark; the stage alone is light; and here the light is dim, as of approaching eventide.

Hullingham and Braiser stand blankly gazing into each other's face, white with fear, not daring to admit, even to themselves, the thoughts that surge madly through their brains. Only the tightening of Sir Carlos' hand on the doctor's arm, and Braiser's trembling, reveal to each the other's fear. Both have recognised the room and the figure of the nurse.

The light darkens slowly, slowly, till all is in a dense and shadowy gloom through the ever-rising and ever-thickening vapour.

Suddenly a mysterious luminance arises from a distant corner of the stage—a glowing radiance, amber, roseate, which grows and grows until, from the depths of a filmy cloud, there comes another figure—a figure clad in diaphanous robes of light, the luminous draperies of the spirit-world.

Nearly to her feet fall the wondrous masses of her red-gold hair; her lovely face is full of a haunting sadness, the wistful, starlike eyes instinct with a world of pain. Tall, with a slow and stately tread, she advances, and pauses in the centre of the stage, majestic in a deathless grandeur of despair. Then a voice of thrilling sweetness—a voice which unites every person in that audience of more than three hundred souls in sympathy, and brings to each the thought, 'It is a spirit from the tomb':

'Mora—Mora Alderson! Carlos, are you here?'

The figure is that of Adelaide Hullingham.

CHAPTER X
A PHANTOM RECITAL: THE 'CONFESSION'

IN a voice as of a sobbing wind, Adelaide Hullingham speaks: 'I, who speak to you, am dead.

'Ten years ago a crime was committed; until it is unveiled, and the criminals exposed, my sprit may not rest. Ten years ago I was the helpless victim of a cruel martyrdom and of a foul conspiracy—a felony by which I met my death. Until my Recital is concluded, I ask that everyone may hold his peace.

'On earth, to man, I was known as Adelaide Milroy Hullingham. I was that helpless woman, the first wife of Sir Carlos Hullingham, the Master of Hullingham Manor. I never possessed my husband's love, although I loved him with an all-consuming passion.

'In 1877 we made the acquaintance of a beautiful girl, whose name was Mora Alderson. She was ethereally lovely—a brunette with hazel eyes. From the hour he saw her first, my husband, Carlos, loved her, and she returned his love.

'A year passed by, and we saw her not; but in 1878 we met her once again in London, and Sir Carlos invited her to Hullingham Manor. In vain I begged him to reconsider the idea, and at his dictation my note to her was written.

'Miss Alderson came, and my husband commanded me to make her welcome, and, as always, I obeyed.

'Till now, his manner to me had, from the first, been simply cold, indifferent, though, in my heart, my love for him burned within me as a living coal. His indifference turned to hate, to bitter hatred, as his love for Miss Alderson grew stronger day by day.

'Soon Miss Alderson was all in all at Hullingham Manor, as she was to him. My children grew to love her—my servants, too. Even I myself could scarcely help but love her, though jealousy consumed me with burning pangs; she had such a winsome manner, so fascinating, that all who knew her were drawn to her in love. She was so young, too, and seemingly so innocent—so blinded by her love for Carlos that she seemed not to see the wrong she did me by that love. In spite of the agony of mind I suffered, I could not help but pity her, for in the end, poor child! she sinned from love. She was but a child in years, and so lovely—so very, very lovely! I could not wonder at Carlos' infatuation.

'Many visits Mora paid us, ever invited by affectionate notes from me, written under pressure of my husband's threats.

'So things went on, until the day came in which I read my doom. On every hand I was slighted, except by Miss Alderson herself, who ever behaved as though she loved me; yet this child was set above me in my home.

'At last the time came when she was looked upon as one of ourselves; and the love grew between her and Sir Carlos, and her child was born. My husband bade me pass him off before the world as mine; at my peril I must obey. A lovely boy, with a brilliant Spanish beauty—olive skin, brown eyes, and raven hair, with cheeks like two round rosy apples. They called him by a pretty Greek name—Edonè. The child grew, and their love for him was wonderful.

'And now it was that my martyrdom began. I was banished. Two rooms were prepared for me in the northern wing, a part of the house in partial ruin, and unused, shut off from the rest by a heavy oaken door, of which my husband, Carlos, kept the key.

'The walls of these rooms were damp and gruesome; blotches of evil-smelling mildew, green and grey, adorned the tattered paper. An odour, as of decay, was in the air; and from the windows the view was obscured, of woods and distant city, by an overgrowth of creepers and of giant trees. The branches tapped at the casements with a ghostly sound.

'Here for many months I lived, a prisoner under lock and key, and only joined the household for my meals.

'It soon became apparent to me that some mystery was going on, for I noted that on the faces of my children and of the servants a curious expression came when I appeared—a look as of pitying wonder. My husband had given out that I was going mad!

'One day I was released from my prison in the northern wing, and informed that I might resume my duties in the household, which since my imprisonment had fallen to my eldest daughter, Lilian. Needless to say, I was surprised and pleased.

'Miss Alderson had left the house: hence my freedom.

'A few months later she returned, and this time came for good. My husband had informed her that my health was so precarious that it was considered necessary that I should keep my room, and he begged her to come and live at Hullingham as companion to my children. With the consent of her aunt, she accepted, and I once more was banished. It was now an open secret that I was going mad, although not sufficiently insane to leave my home. All, even my children, were forbidden to come near me, and by everyone at Hullingham I was supposed to be still a prisoner in the northern wing; but I was no longer there.

A change took place from now in Sir Carlos' treatment of me: I was imprisoned in the "vaulted room." On learning I was to be incarcerated there, so great a horror came over me that I knelt to my husband and craved his pity. He coldly laughed and led me there. This vaulted room was a disused studio, a tent-shaped structure of brick in the garden, apart from the house, but overlooked by the windows of my husband's room and those of that adjoining, which we called "Laurie's room," as it was always given to my brother-in-law Laurence when staying in the house. This apartment was connected with my husband's room by a communicating door, and was now used by Miss Alderson.

'My prison was damp, and like a mildewed dungeon. The floor was slated, the walls cemented, and the drops stood thick upon them. The only window was a small square opening in the northern wall, devoid of glass, through which the wind blew and the rain splashed, and in all the years I spent there I never saw the sun. There was no fireplace in this deadly vault, in which the cold penetrated night and day. Its only furniture, an iron bedstead, a wash-hand-stand, and a single wooden chair. No books were allowed to me, no work, no clock by which to count the passing hours.

'At the bottom of the garden, not far away, there ran a canal which joined the River Thames, and when the river's tide was high the canal would rise, and through a drain or some such opening flood my vault, until the water lay thick upon the floor.

'Into this loathsome dungeon I, Adelaide Hullingham, was cast, and the door locked upon me by my husband Carlos. Here for eight long years I lived and pined, and all but died, my food brought to me by my husband twice a day—prison fare. And so things went on, till in very truth I was well-nigh truly mad. Many rats came up from the canal; I could see their cruel eyes gleaming in the darkness of the night. When the waters were deep upon the floor, I was perforce obliged to keep my bed. Of the years as they passed I lost all count, and verily I took but little note, for I knew now that Carlos hoped to kill me, and for his sake I prayed to die.

'At last a day arrived when I was released from my cruel tomb; and this is how it came about:

'My nerves were shattered, my body weakened, so that I grew fearful of the slightest sound, even of the well-known trickling of the water round my bed, the scurrying of the rats, and the drip-drip-dripping of the walls.

'One night—a winter's night and bitter cold—as I was shivering with chattering teeth upon my bed, watching a clear shaft of moonlight shimmer with glistening radiance upon the floor, more rats came in, so many and so fierce, with their savage eyes gleaming in the moonlight, that I fancied they were glaring at me, and one crawled up upon my bed. I shrieked aloud in frenzied terror, and, leaping upon the floor, rushed through the water to where, low upon the wall, a heavy beam of wood rose slantwise to the roof, supporting the cross-beams of the rafters. Up this I climbed in my night dress and bare feet, and sat upon a cross-beam near the roof. I feared that the rats might follow, for one big fellow ran along the beam, but, scared by a movement of my foot, he turned and scuttled down; my nerve was broken, and I screamed, and screamed again, louder and louder than before, until I heard without the welcome sound of voices. A key was turned in my door, and I saw my husband and Miss Alderson. Sir Carlos bade her stay outside, so I think she did not see the condition of my prison. My husband helped me down from the rafter upon which I sat, and they brought me into the house and placed me in Miss Alderson's bed. Then I learnt that she had heard my cries, had roused Sir Carlos, and forced him to come to my assistance.

'After this, for caution's sake, lest Miss Alderson might guess he was driving me to my death, I was allowed a certain amount of comparative freedom, and my heart sank low within me, for I wondered what new terror awaited me. The slightest relaxation of his harshness I had learnt to dread, for it only meant that there was worse to come. Nor in this case were my fears without foundation, and I shudder even now to think of those days that followed. Although comparatively free, my rooms, as before, were in the northern wing, but the partition door was now left open.

'One dismal day, a short time after my release from the vaulted room, Sir Carlos bade me await him in my bedroom in the northern wing, and, alas for me! I knew I must expect a renewal of my sufferings. I preceded him to my room, and while awaiting his presence sat by the window and watched the heavy raindrops coursing each other down the panes, and listened to the tap-tapping of the leafless branches against the glass. The cold chilled me to the bone, for I was never allowed a fire. The wind moaned in the chimney, and I shivered with ineffable dread. My limbs were growing numbed with the penetrating damp, so I rose, and, after pacing to and fro the room to warm my blood, was about to stretch myself upon the bed, when the door opened, and my husband entered, closing it behind him. His face was very cold and stern, and in his eyes a gleam of cruelty shone, seeing which I sighed, and again I prayed to die.

'Sir Carlos placed an upright chair in the centre of the room, and in silence motioned me to take my seat. God forgive him! I little guessed what was to come.

'From a pocket of his coat he took three heavy iron chains and some pieces of strong twine. With one of the chains he fastened my hands behind me to the back of the chair upon which I sat, attaching the links with a bit of string. In like manner my feet were tied to the two front-legs of the chair, till I could move nor hand nor foot. Then, without a word, he left me and went out, locking the door behind him.

'So I passed another month and more.

'Three times a day Sir Carlos would release me to take my meals—once more prison fare, as in the vault. Each time for half an hour I was free, free to pace my room and warm my aching limbs; and then he would return and bind me fast again until the night, when I was free to go to bed, to be bound again each day at dawn.

'Oh, the blessed rest at night, when I could stretch my aching limbs!

'I noticed with a thrill of horror that very soon my food grew less and less. At first I was fed three times a day; then twice; at last it was reduced to once.

'Thus, day by day, and hour after hour, I was doomed to sit alone in chains, and all through those dreary winter's days, through the dusk of twilight into the darkness of the night, until bedtime came, for I was allowed no light.

'Oh, how I longed for death to come! for I was numbed and racked with pain from my changeless, strained position.

'At last there came a day—I shudder to think of it!—when I was not released at all, nor night nor day, nor even fed. Then I knew that this was the beginning of the end indeed, and that I was left to starve. "Carlos, Carlos, may God forgive you!" was my bitter cry.

'Four long nights and four long days no living soul came near me, till I was racked with pain, with fever, and near delirium from want of sleep. The flesh was raw on my wrists and ankles from the rusty iron on the chains; and again and yet again I cried to God, "Oh, let me die!"

'Perhaps I grew hysterical, I know not, but at last I shrieked aloud. I did not mean to do so; involuntarily the cry burst from me, "Will no one help me?"

'Was it providence, I wonder, or was it chance, that my cries were heard? that my door had been left unbarred? I cannot tell, but Carlos had omitted to lock me in, and little Kate, a child of twelve, while playing with Edonè in the corridor, had heard my cry. She turned the handle of my door and peeped in. Seeing me sitting there, she half withdrew in fear, but I called to her.

' "Mother! Is that *you*?" she cried in awestruck tones, as timidly she advanced to my side. Oh, bitter thought! Was I so altered that my own child had failed to know me?

' "Yes, Kitty dear, it is I," I said. "I'm so tired of sitting here alone; stay with me for a moment. Come near and kiss me, Kit; I—I cannot move."

'Half fearful still, she obeyed. Then for the first time she saw the chains, and, with distended eyes, grew pale.

' "Mother!" she cried; "why do you sit here in this cold room without a fire, and—and with those horrid chains?"

' "Don't ask me, Kitty; I have to sit here, dear," was all I said.

' "I see—I see it all!" she cried, and an angry blush suffused her face. "This is father's doing—I know it is. Oh, what a shame! Mother, I'm going to undo these chains, and if father's cross, you may tell him it was I who did it. I'm not one bit afraid of father!" and the brave child loosened the cruel iron which ate into my flesh and pained me so.

'I suppose I must have fainted, for I remember nothing after that, until I found myself upon the bed, a fire blazing in the grate, and my daughters Lilian and Nellie crying by my side, with the younger children, and sitting at the foot of my bed was little Kate. In Kitty's eyes there were no tears, but an expression set and hard, and very sad, unlike the expression of a child—more like to that of a woman who has suffered.

'Once more I was free—a brief respite from my torture. Whether Carlos learnt that Kitty had released me, I know not, but he was afraid to imprison me again.

'Now for the first time, within the days that followed, I felt a strange sensation in my head—a sudden burning, and a faintness which turned me sick. Many times I felt it after this: once as I was descending the stairs, and I was forced to stop, and clutch at the balusters to save myself from falling.

'Another child was born to Carlos and Mora, a wee frail mite— a girl, who only lived a month. I mention this, because what I have to tell will touch upon it.

'A few weeks after my release by Kitty, as I passed the library, the door of which was ajar, I looked in. Concealed myself by the heavy *portière*, I was unnoticed by the persons in the room. And this is what I saw: My husband Carlos was seated at the table, writing. By his side, Mora Alderson—oh, how fair she looked!—was helping him with his work. In the window recess the children were playing: my Nellie, and Mora's Edonè, and little Kate. But Kitty was apart from the rest, and her eyes were fixed in a bewildered stare upon her father and Miss Alderson. Presently Mora clasped her arms round my husband's neck, and kissed him upon the brow—a kiss that I so often would have given, but, alas! well I knew that from me it would have been unwelcome. Miss Alderson alone had power to stir the ardent love of this man to flame, who, in spite of all, I worshipped more than life! As though paralyzed, I stood and watched them—hungrily, with bitter, jealous misery. Carlos looked up at the girl at his side, his eyes aglow with passion, and whispered something I could not hear, but she blushed and smiled. They were so happy in each other's love, their children playing side by side; so happy—ah, so happy! The picture was complete, and I saw that I was not even missed; and then it was that I knew I was one too many in the world. In my heart a bitter cry uprose, "Ah, woe is me! why was I ever born? Oh, let me die! Oh, let me die!" Then once again the burning sickness in my head, and something seemed to crack within my brain, and I felt a flood of giddiness come over me, and I fled screaming down gallery and hall, tearing my hair, which fell in a shower around me as I ran. Carlos and Miss Alderson rushed out from the library, and the children stood with frightened faces in the doorway. Up and down the great oak staircase Miss Alderson and Carlos chased me, and my screaming grew more and more insane, and I knew that now, in very truth, I was mad indeed! At last they caught me, and bound my hands behind me with a pocket-handkerchief, and Sir Carlos carried me, and laid me upon the sofa in the drawing-room, and I heard him despatch a servant for the doctor. He came, and as in the mazes of a dream I heard their words. "Lady Hullingham is mad," the doctor said. Then breathlessly, with my ebbing senses, I listened for my husband's answer. It came, and after it I knew no more: "Her baby's death has sent her mad." May God pardon you, Carlos, for that lie!

*   *   *   *   *

'Five years went by, and one day, as from a dream, I awoke to consciousness, weary, weary, as a little child fresh roused from sleep. Wonderingly, I looked around me. All was strange. I was in a large drawing-room, where were many people. A lady was playing upon a pianoforte; the music jarred my nerves. Through the window by which I sat, and which opened to the ground, men and women passed to and fro. Without was a beautiful garden, with drooping trees, and grass so green and smooth, and far away the glint of water, and they said it was the sea. Every face was strange to me: some were bright, some were wild, and some were sad; but all had a senseless, vacant look which made me shudder. And then, as in a flash, the truth came to me: I was the inmate of a madhouse. Yes, that was it! I had been mad; my senses had returned, and I was sane. Sane! How I laughed, as a happy child, as thought came to me! Alas! my joy was of short duration; for with my recovered intellect memory returned, and I remembered all the torment I had undergone, and the scene that drove me mad. Carlos? Mora? My children—what of them? A thousand questions chased each other through my brain. "Surely now." I thought, "after my madness, Carlos will be kind?" Foolish thought! My hopes, indeed, were soon dispelled. An attendant entered, an asylum nurse, and called me to my tea, which, it seems, I took in my private room. I rose and followed her. My room was small and poorly furnished, as is this, you see. I liked the appearance of my nurse; her face was kind, though rather stern, and her name, I learnt, was Janet Stirling. She had had the charge of me from the first. As she placed my tea before me upon the table, she glanced at me, and I saw her start. Then she looked at me very keenly, and asked if I was well, and then she smiled. The tears rose to my eyes, and I wept, for no one had smiled at me for years and years. I drew her to me and kissed her, and then I saw that the tears were in her eyes also, and from that hour we grew friends.

'I told her how, sitting in the room downstairs, my senses had returned, and I knew I had been mad.

' "How long have I been here?" I asked.

' "Five years."

' "So long?" I cried wistfully. "And—they will set me free. When?"

' "At once. Dr. Braiser will communicate with your husband to-night most probably, and as soon as the usual formalities are concluded you will be free."

'The doctor came to see me, and with many questions examined me minutely, and then he smiled.

' "You are quite well again, Lady Hullingham," he said. "You are as sane as I am. I will send a wire to Sir Carlos now, and I expect he will come for you to-morrow."

'The morrow came, and impatiently I awaited my husband's arrival; but he did not come. Day after day went by, and still he made no sign. What could it mean? I began at last to be filled with a sense of foreboding, and I feared I knew not what!

'A week passed away, and one afternoon I had another visit from Dr. Braiser, who this time was very grave, and shook his head. I wondered what was wrong, but the doctor left me in silence. I took an unreasoning dislike to this man, I know not why. His face to me was so repellent; there was an expression so false, so crafty, in his eyes.

'Days and days passed by, and still my husband made no sign. At last I could bear the suspense no longer, so I wrote to Carlos, imploring him to take me home.

'All this time Nurse Stirling went and came in silence. She seldom spoke to me or glanced my way, and my heart sank low within me for very fear, for her face was hard and stern. When she thought I was not observing, she would watch me closely, and then her face grew harder still.

'Oh, heaven! what could it mean? I was nearly mad with fear!

'One evening, after I had had my tea, I heard angry voices in an adjoining room, which I recognised as those of my nurse and Dr. Braiser. I heard my name, and instinct told me I was the subject of their dispute. I ran to the door and listened, straining every nerve to hear, and though here and there I missed a word, I gathered the sense of all they said. Nurse Stirling was expostulating about some wrong. I heard the words "police" and "unlawful fraud," and then the angry voice of Dr. Braiser said in strident tones: "She's not sane—she's mad!" God! what did he mean? I sank upon my knees by the door, and then I heard what filled my heart with joy, yet mixed with bitter pain.

' "Lady Hullingham is not mad; she is as sane as you or I, Dr. Braiser, and you know it!"

' "Thank God! oh, thank God! At least I have one friend here!" I cried.

' "By what authority do you dare to question my statements, Nurse Stirling?" the doctor cried furiously. "I tell you the woman's mad!"

' "I question your statement on the authority of a qualified lunacy nurse," said Miss Stirling calmly. "In Lady Hullingham there is no trace of insanity. You are laying yourselves open to arrest for conspiracy, you and Sir Carlos Hullingham."

'I started up. Could I have heard aright? Sir Carlos Hullingham! Sir Carlos Hullingham! Conspiracy! Oh, in God's name, what did it mean? Then I wonder that I retained my sanity, for slowly the truth dawned on me, and I realized that my husband had conspired with Dr. Braiser to keep me here as mad. "Wretched, wretched woman that I am!" I cried, with bitter wailing. "Why, oh why, was I ever born?"

'The days went by, and Nurse Stirling's face was black as night, and at last I prevailed upon her to tell me all.

' "At least, let me know the worst," I cried; "death is preferable to waiting from day to day like this!"

'At first she was reticent, and would tell me nothing; but my passionate pleadings and her indignation at the wrong that was being done to me at length overcame her scruples, and she confessed the truth.

' "Dr. Braiser denies your sanity," she said. "Your husband has bribed him to retain you here as insane. Their action is a felony. I know that what I state is true, for a week ago Sir Carlos Hullingham came here, and was——"

' "Carlos," I cried, "came here and—and I did not see him? Nurse Stirling!"

' "He was closeted with the doctor for upwards of an hour, and as he went away I happened to be passing through the hall, and heard their words as the doctor saw him out. As I passed behind them in my soft shoes, they did not hear or see me, and, guessing something of the sort, I paused on the turn of the staircase, and listened to what they said. Thinking themselves alone, they spoke aloud, and this is what I heard:

' " 'Remember,' said Sir Carlos, 'a word, and it's gaol for both of us.'

' " 'Never fear,' said Braiser; 'she's mad from now on.'

' " 'All right, old man; I'll send you cash, as a cheque might betray us.'

' "That was enough for me. That night I charged the doctor with his crime, and threatened to expose him unless justice was done to you; and he said he would consider it, then grew white as death, and all but struck me."

'One day, a few days after this, the door of my room opened, and my husband stood before me. I sprang from my chair with joy.

' "You have come at last! Carlos! husband! take me from this fearful place! See, I am quite sane now."

' "Yes; you are cured," he said.

'No word of love or greeting after all these years! He stood by the door, with his hat in his hand, and on his face an icy smile. I felt as turned to stone, yet once again I cried: "Will you not set me free? Oh, Carlos, take me home!"

' "Your presence at Hullingham Manor is undesired; but you will regain your freedom soon."

'And with that he left me.

'Four weary months went by, and once again he stood before me, colder and haughtier than before. I knelt to him and begged him, with scalding tears, to set me free. I seized his hand, but he flung me from him as though I had been an adder. Then I said: "What wrong have I ever done you, Carlos, that you should be so cruel? I bore those years of torment at your hands without a murmur. Have mercy, and let me go free! If my presence at home is so unwelcome, let me go away—far away, where no one will know me—where I may never see you, to cause you pain; only take me from this madhouse, which is a terror to me, worse than any I have borne. I feel that if I stay here I shall go mad again! Oh, set me free! I am only a poor, miserable, helpless woman, Carlos—truly, the most miserable woman that was ever born, and I would never, never harm you!"

"I cannot trust you," he answered coldly. "You stand between me and the woman I love; but for your cursed existence she would be my wife. I hate you; you—you are in my way! Now do you understand?"

'With a low cry, I covered my face with my hands and sobbed, "Yes, yes! I understand. You will never set me free. I must remain here until I die. Carlos, may God forgive you!"

' "You will regain your freedom soon."

'With that he went away.

'I watched him close the door; then, as in a dream, I walked to the window and looked out upon the trees and lawn. I knew my doom. I, Adelaide Hullingham, a sane woman, must remain here, a prisoner in a madhouse, until I died. Yes, yes! I saw it all quite plainly now, and as I turned back from the window to the dreary room, my cage from henceforth, my heart was broken.

'So I lived on, and, like the poor imprisoned bird, beat my wings against the bars in vain.

'During these day of misery my friendship grew for Sister Janet Stirling. Day after day she threatened to expose the conspiracy which kept me here; but at my earnest prayer, for Carlos' sake, she desisted, for, as I said, wherever I was I must be done to death. On one condition, and one alone, she consented to hold her tongue, though greatly against her will. This condition was that I should write a full and detailed account or confession of the conspiracy, and of every single act of cruelty perpetrated upon me at Hullingham in the past by my husband, Carlos, withholding nothing, on my solemn oath. Failing this, she would lay the facts of all she knew before the police at Scotland Yard. For Carlos' sake, in the end, I complied, and wrote the full confession of my martyrdom to Miss Mora Alderson, and signed it with my name as the truth, the whole truth, and nothing but the truth, so help me God.

'This confession was delivered to Mora Alderson after my death by Janet Stirling. At the conclusion, before I signed my name, I wrote these words: "I forgive you, Mora Alderson, poor sinful child; you sinned from love, and knew not the wrong you did me by that love. Marry Carlos when I am dead, and let not my dark shadow cross your path. Pity me not, for in paradise I shall have found the joy denied me on earth, and in your perfect happiness forget that Adelaide Milroy Hullingham ever lived. Farewell; I forgive you freely, both you and Carlos, my beloved husband; may God as easily forgive!"

'Thus ended the confession.

*   *   *   *   *

'At last there came a day when I knew that the end was near, and that I was dying. The doors of my prison would soon be opened now, and I should at last be free—released by the angel Death!

'But as I lay upon my bed there came to me a longing, a passionate yearning, once more to look upon the house which held the man so cruel, yet so madly worshipped, who was killing me; once more to hold my children in my arms—my daughters Lilian, Nellie, and little Kate. Surely they would be sorry for me if they knew of the agony I have undergone, and pity their most miserable mother. But they do not know, and 'tis sure they never will, for, if left to Carlos, the secret of my death and martyrdom will be kept until the end. I longed once more to look upon the sea—the blue expanse of ocean, with its ever-changing swell; to see the trees, green fields, and downs again, and breathe the pure air of heaven; but 'twas not to be. I was dying; my head was on fire, burning, throbbing with nauseous pain which drew me lower, lower in my bed to death, in ever-increasing agony—greater, greater, until suddenly it ceased! Oh, the blessed sensation of rest, of peace, which followed. Was it death? I wondered. No, not yet; for, as in a mist, I saw the form of Mora Alderson beside my bed, and Lily, Nellie, Kitty, and my sons—all, all were there save my husband, Carlos. Where was he? Why did he not come? Presently I felt the arms of Mora Alderson around me. She kissed me, and murmured through her tears, poor child: "Adelaide—for—forgive! Forgive!" I whispered back in a voice as though from far away: "I—I for—give. God—pardon—you and —him! Fare—well!"

'As in a maze, the voices whispered round me as all the world grew dark, and I was sinking—sinking—when I heard the word "meningitis," and I knew from what I died. And then the word thundered and thundered through my brain with every decreasing

80

heart-beat: men-in-gitis! Then Janet Stirling kissed me, and murmured in my deafening ears: "Adelaide, you will be avenged!" They were the last words I heard on earth: in a moment I was dead.

*   *   *   *   *

'My recital is concluded.

'Until this crime was to the world unveiled, my spirit could not rest. With you shall lie the judgment. The criminals both are present—Sir Carlos Hullingham and Dr. Richard Braiser—in your midst. Deal with them in equity and justice, and may God have mercy upon their souls, for on earth they can expect but retribution!

'Fare ye well; and pray that my spirit may find rest.'

*   *   *   *   *

With a sobbing sign, as the gauzy folds of a dense and pulsating vapour enfold her, she vanishes, and the crimson curtains fall.

*   *   *   *   *

No sound breaks the stillness for quite a minute—every heart is too full for speech; and the lights are raised to a gentle music, which fills the rooms as an accompaniment to the thoughts that run through every mind.

CHAPTER XI
RETRIBUTION

THE scene which follows baffles all description, and for the nonce Lady Mountjoy's house is chaos. The guests for the time forget that they are aristocrats, and remember only that they are men—men and women who have been duped, insulted, betrayed; who have harboured in their midst, honoured and adored, a felon, a murderer, a very fiend in human guise, for whom no earthly punishment can be too severe. A cry is raised of 'Police! police! We are not safe while such a demon is at large!' The babel of tongues is deafening, the excitement at boiling pitch. The hubbub is so immense that the arrest of Braiser takes place unnoticed, and the criminal has left the house before anyone is aware that he has gone. All is accomplished in perfect order and silence, so as to save unpleasantness to the lady of the house.

Shortly after the departure of the doctor, Lord Dartmoor approaches Sir Carlos Hullingham, where he sits beneath the palms. He is accompanied by a stranger, a gentleman in evening dress, whose name is Henderson; he is a detective from Scotland Yard. In a courteous tone he addresses Sir Carlos, requesting a private interview below. The Baronet does not stir. His head is buried in his hands, his elbows upon his knees, his eyes fixed in an unseeing stare. Surprised at receiving no answer, the detective touches him on the arm, but still he does not move. Then Mr. Henderson looks up at his companion, and both men grow alarmed.

'Hullingham! Are you ill? Speak, man, and tell us what is wrong,' says Lord Dartmoor, concerned.

But the Baronet does not stir.

The young man shrugs his shoulders as he turns to the detective.

'I don't know what's the matter with him,' he say. 'Stay here, will you, while I hunt up her ladyship. Perhaps there's a doctor here.'

'Very good, my lord; I'll stay,' says Henderson.

Lord Dartmoor spies his hostess across the room, and shoulders his way in her direction. The gravity of his face as he comes up to her warns her that something is amiss.

'What's wrong?' she asks. 'You're worried. What is it?'

'Well, the fact is, Hullingham's ill. Is there a doctor here, or can I send for one?'

Lady Mountjoy looks frightened.

'Ill? Sir Carlos? What's the matter with him?'

'I can't say,' says Dartmoor gloomily. 'Seems stunned, and don't speak.'

'Well, if he's not gone, Sir Thornton Bramwell's here. You go back to Sir Carlos, and I'll seek him out. Probably he's in the supper-room;' and she goes in search of the great physician, while Lord Dartmoor rejoins the detective and Hullingham.

'It's very strange,' says Henderson as Dartmoor comes up to them; 'I suppose it's the shock from the exposure of his crime. He doesn't seem to understand anything I say to him.'

Presently they observe their hostess approaching through the crowd, accompanied by Sir Thornton Bramwell and Nurse Stirling.

Sir Thornton is a big man, about sixty years of age, perhaps a little younger, with gray hair and a silvered beard, that once was fair. He has a genial manner, rather pompous, and a kindly smile.

One glance at the Baronet is enough. He strokes his beard and shakes his head, and exchanges a look with the nurse.

'Total paralysis! Sir Carlos Hullingham may live for years, but he will never move or speak again. What a frightful retribution! Get him home as quickly as you can.'

'I will take him home, an stay with him till another nurse can come,' says Janet Stirling.

'Thank you, Janet,' Lady Mountjoy says simply; 'I could not rest unless I knew that someone would see to that wretched man's safety. Considering all things, it is good of you to offer,' she adds in a lower tone.

'It is my duty as the only nurse present,' Janet retorts a little sharply.

'I will send a nurse to Hullingham Manor by to-morrow morning,' says Sir Thornton. 'A terrible story we have heard to-night; but it's well the truth is told. One doesn't like to be duped. It makes one feel so—so foolish!' he adds with a smile. 'And now I must be going. Good-night to you, Lady Mountjoy.'

Lord Dartmoor had gone to order the stricken Baronet's carriage, and now he returns, with two servants, who carry Sir Carlos away between them, followed by Lady Mountjoy and Nurse Stirling, with Lord Dartmoor.

'Where's Dr. Braiser?' asks her ladyship uneasily, glancing around.

'Gone,' says Janet quickly. 'They have taken him to Scotland Yard. I laid the charge before the authorities there to-day, told them of the projected Recital and the presence of the criminals, and they arranged to send a couple of detectives in evening dress, to take them, if necessary. Mr. Henderson was in the act of arresting Sir Carlos Hullingham when it was found that he was ill.'

At this moment Lord Mountjoy comes up to them. He looks harassed and weary.

'Everyone is unanimous, Bertha,' he says, 'in their cry for justice.

It is most distressing; but we must send for the police and give them up. This affair has upset me more than I can say. Hullingham was such a special friend of ours. It's really very horrible!'

'The police have taken Dr. Braiser, Mountjoy,' says his wife. 'There were two detectives present at the Recital. As for Sir Carlos— poor fellow!—he has passed beyond all earthly judgment. He is— paralyzed; he—he will never speak again.'

'Good God, Bertha!' cries his lordship, aghast; 'paralyzed? Hullingham? Poor fellow! poor fellow! And only an hour or so ago he entered this room, the very picture of perfect manhood! It's too horrible, really! It almost looks like retribution!'

    *   *   *   *   *

Arrived at Hullingham Manor—for it is within a drive from town—the master's return as a helpless cripple comes to the servants and the faithful Rowlands with the effect of a thunderbolt.

He is carried direct to the library, where a bright fire awaits him, and is laid in his favourite easy-chair—the same in which he sat when, at the commencement of this story, we saw him first, in the zenith of his vigorous health; now—paralyzed! Truly, life is a mystery! Who can tell what a day may bring forth?

A servant is despatched riding for the doctor, who lives not far away; and while she waits, Nurse Stirling kneels upon the rug before the fire at the feet of the helpless man. She scans his marble countenance, beautiful as a statue in its fixed rigidity, but for the staring eyes, which are rather horrifying.

Somehow, after the confession, recited, as it was to-night, apparently by the spirit of the dead, as she realizes that for the first time in her life she is beneath the roof of the very house in which Adelaide lived and suffered, alone in the company of the man who killed her, strong woman though she is, she shudders. Her nerves are shaken; she fears she knows not what. An incomprehensible, an intangible fear oppresses her, and involuntarily her heart quickens its beat, and her eyes are persistently drawn to the silent figure in the chair. How like a corpse he looks—immovable, rigid as the dead, with wide, unseeing eyes staring fixedly before him! The ghostly room, the heavy tapestries, the horror of the remembrance of her friend's tortures in this house—all strain her nerves to highest tension. She looks around.

'The library!' she exclaims aloud. 'In this very room, then, the scene took place which drove her mad! There's the table at which Sir Carlos sat, with Mora Alderson beside him! There, the window where the children played! A glorious old house, but, oh, how full of horror!'

Her nerves seem strangely out of tune to-night, for it seems to her that she can hear the sound of voices, and Adelaide's voice, as she heard it last at the asylum—and again she shivers. To turn her thoughts, she watches the quiet figure in the chair, and ponders upon the varying forms of this fell disease, paralysis; and presently she shudders.

'Perhaps the ears are open to hear,' she thinks, 'the heart alive to suffer, yet the body incapable of showing pain. Who can tell? What science yet has penetrated the terrific possibilities of this terrible disease? Who can tell but that, notwithstanding the rigidity of the body, the mind is clear? that memory, remorse, love, hatred, jealousy—every passion of the mind and heart—are not alert and living; nay, doubly, trebly living, from the atrophy of the physical frame? An awful thought. But who can tell that it is not true? Where is the scientist who has solved this problem? How know we but that Sir Carlos Hullingham is alive to all that is going on around him, yet can make no sign; can hear, but cannot speak; can feel, but cannot move or show his sense of pain? Who can tell? Even the eye is fixed, as the hands and feet, in a marble immobility. If there be not insensibility of mind, then indeed, to Sir Carlos Hullingham, his doom is retribution!'

The thought of such a dire possibility thrills her heart with a wave of pity for the stricken man. She rises slowly to her feet, and then a cry bursts from her, for, from the wall above her head, the eyes of Adelaide Hullingham are gazing into hers with all their haunting sorrow. The pictured face looks strangely real to-night, and through their mist of tears the blue eyes seem to smile. Scanning the well-known features of the portrait, Nurse Stirling's thoughts fly back to the weird Recital and its tragic ending, and her wonder grows.

'How could Lady Hullingham have so transformed herself as to become the living, breathing image of this picture of the dead?'

It is a mystery she cannot solve. One day, perhaps, she will know. Her thoughts are interrupted by the entrance of the doctor, and it is with distinct relief that she clasps the hand of the brisk young surgeon.

Dr. Morecombe starts as his eyes rest on Sir Carlos, and his face grows grave. After a brief examination, like Sir Thornton Bramwell, he shakes his head.

'Total paralysis, mental and physical. God in His mercy grant he may die soon! A fearful doom—half a lifetime locked in the rigidity of death! Someone must stay with him night and day. Are you his nurse?'

'No. He happened to be at a reception given at a house where I was staying, and I offered to bring him home and stay till a nurse can come. By a happy chance, Sir Thornton Bramwell, the great specialist, was there, and promised to send a nurse to-morrow. His wife will most likely return then, too.'

'I'm glad indeed to hear that! They have been separated too long already. Of course, she was right to leave him as things were, but a calamity such as this o'ersteps all earthly quarrels. Poor fellow! he will need some loving care, although unconscious of it. What a loss to the world, where he has shone so long, a brilliant star!'

'H'm!' says Nurse Stirling, 'that's as may be.'

Dr. Morecombe stares at her in wonder, but she says no more. After a few words as to the patient's treatment, he takes his leave. When he has gone, Nurse Stirling goes up to the old butler, Rowlands, as he chains up the door.

'Is Miss—Miss Reine Donati here?' she asks.

'Yes, miss; she returned shortly after midnight; she is in her room.'

'Has she retired for the night, or is she awaiting Sir Carlos' return? Do you know?'

'I don't think she's retired, miss; she mostly waits up for the master when he's out late. I wonder she's not been down.'

'Will you send and ask her to come and speak to me in the library, please, if she is up?'

'In the library, miss?' asks Rowlands.

'Yes.'

Janet re-enters the room and closes the door. In a few minutes the actress comes in, but, seeing a stranger, pauses. She is attired in a clinging drapery of pale-green Indian silk, which scarce conceals the voluptuous outlines of her form. Her raven tresses are unbound and fall as a dusky veil around her, exhaling a wizard perfume, and a cluster of tea-roses is fastened at her neck.

In sending up Nurse Stirling's message, Rowlands had slightly altered its wording, stating that Sir Carlos desired her presence in the library. No other words, he rightly knew, would bring her down.

Noticing that the stranger is a hospital nurse, and glancing at her lover, with a cry of terror Reine Donati leaps forward, falling upon her knees beside him.

'Carlo! Carlo!' she cries, as she brushes her hair impatiently from her eyes, 'are you ill? Speak! speak, my darling! Tell me what is wrong!'

The Baronet answers not a word. To all appearance, he is lifeless.

'Are you Miss Reine Donati?' Nurse Stirling asks, standing by the sick man's chair, and icily regarding the prostrate girl at her feet.

The Creole rises, her head thrown proudly back, as she stares at the nurse in cold disdain. 'I am Miss Donati—yes'—in a tone which makes Janet smile. 'What, may I ask, is the meaning of your presence here? If he is ill, can Sir Carlos Hullingham not answer for himself?'

Her breath comes fast and her bosom heaves, as a sense of foreboding falls upon her.

'Sir Carlos Hullingham will never speak again; he is paralyzed.'

'Paralyzed?' she cries hoarsely. 'Oh, my God!'

'I sent for you,' Nurse Stirling goes on, ignoring her bitter cry, 'in order to inform you that, in the absence of Lady Hullingham, I am invested with full authority in this house until she returns to-morrow. You understand?'

A shiver is the actress's only answer.

'Before ten o'clock to-morrow, in her name, I request that you will have left the house. Your presence here is an insult to me and any honest woman. I don't wish to see you again, but as the hour is late to-night, you may stay until the morning. That is all I have to say. You can go. I shall stay with Sir Carlos Hullingham.'

With a glance of rage and baffled passion at Sir Carlos and the nurse, she turns in silence and proudly leaves the room. She is no fool, and, seeing the state of affairs, she knows that the nurse has power to have her forcibly ejected.

Before eight next morning she has gone!

So is the Manor rid of the shameful presence of Reine Donati, and the way made clear for Lady Hullingham's return.

As soon as the door has closed behind the actress, Nurse Stirling rings the bell.

'You are the butler?'—as Rowlands enters.

'Yes, miss,' and his eyes light up with pleasure at the sight of her honest face. He and all the servants at the Manor have had as much as they can stand of such as Reine Donati.

'Very well,' says Nurse Stirling; 'to you, as head of the servants, I will speak as to all. I doubt not it will give you pleasure to learn that this—this person, Miss Donati, will have left this house before ten o'clock to-morrow morning, and that in the course of the day your mistress, Lady Hullingham, will return to take her place at her husband's side; am I not right?' she adds with a smile.

'Missie comes back to-morrow? Oh, thank God! thank God!' And the old servant's eyes are wet with tears of joy.

'I remain with Sir Carlos till your mistress and another nurse arrive to take my place. Until then, by Lady Hullingham's desire, you will take your orders from me.'

'Willingly indeed, Miss Stirling, and I speak for one and all,' says Rowlands huskily.

'Thank you,' says Janet gently. 'Now, before you go to bed, there is one thing more I wish to say. You knew your master's first wife, Adelaide?'

'If I knew "Miss Adelaide"? God rest her soul! I've been butler in this family for thirty years, Miss Stirling; and their interest is to me as my own.'

'Then, you knew your late mistress died in a private asylum for the insane?'

'Yes, miss, I knew that.'

'Well, Rowlands, I was her nurse at the asylum; and before she died I became her friend.'

'Is that so indeed, Miss Stirling? Then, I'm honoured to serve you, ma'am!'

'Lady Hullingham was the victim of an odious crime, a felony, which to-night has been exposed. Lady Hullingham was not a madwoman when she died. For fourteen months before her death, from inflammation of the brain, she was as sane as you or I! She was done to death by a cruel fraud, and her murderer was her husband—your master, Sir Carlos Hullingham! Listen.'

In a few words Janet relates the outlines of the miserable story.

'It is better you should hear the fact from me, before you read it in the newspapers to-morrow morning,' she says, in conclusion.

'And—and that doctor, miss?' the old man cries in burning indignation.

'He is in prison: he was arrested after the Recital.'

'Sarve 'im right, miss! Hangin' 's too good for the likes 'o him! Poor mistress! Poor, dear mistress!'

'And what of the man who killed her, who bribed the doctor—your master, Carlos Hullingham?' And she glances at the figure in the chair.

Rowlands looks uncomfortable, and fumbles with his watch-chain.

'Well, miss, I—I can't say, indeed. Master is—well, you see, miss, master's Sir Carlos!'—desperately.

Nurse Stirling smiles.

'There speaks the faithful servant, the truest friend! Your master has been a grievous sinner—cruel alike both to the living and the dead; a criminal of the lowest type: but his case has been taken by a higher than an earthly court, and his punishment he has received.

He is paralyzed: he will never speak again. It is retribution!'

'Retribution?' cries Rowlands, starting violently. 'Good gracious me, it's New Year's Eve! Tell me, tell me, Miss Stirling, at what hour was he, master, stricken down?' And the butler, in his excitement, lays his hand upon her arm.

'At the stroke of midnight, the hour in which his crime was revealed.'

For the time she had forgotten the superstition of the Hullinghams, and the remembrance makes present events the more appalling.

'You are right, Miss Stirling,' Rowlands says, with great solemnity. 'It is the hand of God: it is retribution!'

His face is deathly pale as he glances at Sir Carlos, and he trembles.

Suddenly with a flash the electric lights go out, and, save for the embers' glow, the room is in darkness.

Is it fancy? but to the butler and the nurse it seems that, around the silent figure of Sir Carlos Hullingham, the shadows are densely peopled with filmy forms, and that the air resounds with the ghostly cry of 'Retribution! Retribution!'

CHAPTER XII
ADELAIDE'S AVENGING

To return to Mora. No sooner is her Recital concluded than, flinging on her cloak and veil, she hurries from the room through a door behind the platform.

In the hall she begs a servant to seek out Frank Hullingham, as she is tired, and wants to go straight home. While waiting she sits at the entrance to the supper-room, her luminous draperies and 'make-up' concealed by her cloak and veil.

Strangely weary and out of sorts she feels; and there is a painful oppression in her chest, which impedes her breathing, producing a sensation as of asphyxia.

Presently she sees her nephew approaching down the stairs, accompanied by Nurse Stirling.

'You're done up,' says the nurse brusquely. 'You had better let your nephew take you home at once, and I will follow later with the others.'

She asks a servant to call a cab and get a glass of champagne for Mademoiselle Mora.

'I'm afraid this has been too much for you, Aunt Mora,' says young Hullingham, concerned. 'I hope you won't be ill.'

Mora smiles.

'I shall be glad to get away,' she says. 'I don't feel well.'

'Ah, here comes Aunt Patience and Miss Heywood. That's nice; we shall be able to get away together, after all,' says Frank, relieved.

At this moment Miss Gabrielle Rayburn approaches along the hall from the boudoir, and addresses Nurse Stirling.

'Can you speak a word to my aunt, Miss Stirling, before you go?' she says. 'She's in the boudoir.'

'Yes, I'll come,' Janet replies; and together they proceed to the little room.

'Janet,' says Lady Mountjoy, who is speaking to the great physician, Sir Thornton Bramwell, as they enter, 'Sir Carlos Hullingham is ill; will you come with us to him? You know Sir Thornton Bramwell? Sister Janet Stirling'—introducing her.

Sending a message by a passing servant, as they ascend the stairs, to Frank Hullingham, she accompanies Lady Mountjoy and the doctor to the drawing-room.

    *   *   *   *   *

Arrived at their lodgings, in a street not far away, Lady Hullingham sinks upon a couch, throwing off her cloak and veil, and appears once more in her shining draperies and paint.

'Hadn't you better go straight to bed? You look worn out, Aunt Mora,' says Frank Hullingham, as he takes her cloak.

He regards her anxiously, for her breathing is so oppressed. Trying to rise, she falls back exhausted, and complains of pain in her throat and side.

'Give me some brandy, Patience, please,' she murmurs wearily, as she presses her hand to her eyes. 'There's some in that flask on the sideboard. Thank you. Now help me up; I feel as if I should fall.'

'What a nuisance Nurse Stirling isn't here!' cries Frank desperately. 'Perhaps I'd better fetch a doctor, for I'm afraid you're ill, Aunt Mora.'

'Oh no,' she answers, smiling; 'I shall be better after a night's rest. Good-night, Frank. Come, Lucy and Patience.'

Next morning Mora seems worse, having passed a restless night; but she has risen, for she is anxious to return to Rottingdean. It requires but little acumen to see that she is very seriously indisposed, for she complains of a growing pain in her side, and a difficulty in swallowing. So pale is she that she looks almost as ghostly as upon the platform the night before.

Anxiously watching her, Hullingham's face grows suddenly grave, as though from a passing thought.

'I don't think the amount of phosphorous you must have inhaled has done you any good, Aunt Mora,' he says quietly.

'Oh, that's nothing. I shall be all right soon. I'm only overdone, and my nerves a bit strained; I feel on the verge of hysterics. When can we get away?'

'There's a train at three; can you be ready to catch that?'

'Yes;' and she seems relieved.

Then they talk of other things—of the Recital.

'How did you contrive to get your face and voice so exact to the original of the late Lady Hullingham, Mora?' asks Lucy. 'I heard on all sides the likeness was uncannily precise.'

'Nurse Stirling said she was horribly startled when she saw you first in that "get-up"; and as for me, well—I never saw anything like it. You were the living image of Aunt Adelaide,' says Frank. 'How did you do it?'

'A natural gift of mimicry and a little paint—besides high heels and a wig. The make-up was nothing; the hardest part of all was the voice. You have no idea what an effort it was, in spite of terrible emotion, to maintain that muffled tone for an hour or more without a pause. It was frightfully fatiguing.'

At this moment the double knock of a telegraph-boy startles them, and Mora turns pale. She presses her hand to her side as if in pain, and a blue tinge encircles her mouth.

'How weak I am!' she thinks contemptuously. 'Perhaps it isn't for us at all.'

In a minute more the lodging maid-of-all-work enters, and hands an orange envelope to Frank, who tears it open.

'No answer,' he says, and the girl withdraws.

The hearts of the three women are beating wildly, for the message can but come from Nurse Stirling, for no one else knows their address. Mora's face is white, and she trembles.

'Carlos is ill; I know it,' she cries hoarsely.

'You are right, Aunt Mora. The wire is from Miss Stirling, from Hullingham Manor. There—read it for yourself.'

And she reads as follows:

'Sir Carlos ill. Bring Lady H. at once. Miss R. D. gone. I am here.
'JANET STIRLING.'

'Come,' she cries; 'I shall go at once. Will you come with me, Frank?'

'Of course, Aunt Mora. You ladies had better remain here till I return in the course of the day—unless you prefer to catch the three o'clock train to Rottingdean?'

'No. We'll stop here till you come back, and then we can arrange our future plans,' says Patience.

*　　　*　　　*　　　*　　　*

In the hall at Hullingham Manor, Frank and Mora are met by Janet Stirling, who takes Mora's hand and kisses her.

'Welcome home, Lady Hullingham!' she says with a smile. 'Will you both come to the dining-room, please? Before you see your husband, Lady Hullingham, I must speak to you.'

They enter the room and close the door. Mora turns to the nurse, and her lips are trembling.

'My husband? Speak, Nurse Stirling! I—I can bear anything but suspense. He—is—dead?' and she leans heavily upon her nephew's arm.

'Your Husband is ill, Lady Hullingham, but not dangerously so; that is to say, he may live for years. You are not well. Sit down. Before I tell you a word more, you must have some brandy.'

There are glasses, brandy, and a syphon on the table. Janet mixes a glass and hands it to Mora, who drinks it with shaking hands. Frank and the nurse cross the room to the window.

'When did she get like this?' asks Janet in a low tone.

'Last night on her return home. I can't say how we regretted your absence. I don't understand it at all; she seems to get no better.'

'H'm!' grunts Nurse Stirling, but she says nothing. She watches Lady Hullingham intently, for there is a look on her face which alarms the nurse; the blue round her mouth is spreading, and her breathing seems more laboured. Janet moves up to her.

'You must be brave, Lady Hullingham,' she says gently, 'and prepare yourself for a shock. You wished for retribution in making public Adelaide's confession. You have your wish; your husband, Sir Carlos Hullingham, is—paralyzed.'

'Good God!' cries Frank, sinking on to a chair. 'Poor devil!'

In moments of excitement he is his father's son, who ever called a spade a spade.

Mora's face is blanched with horror.

'Paralyzed! Carlos? No, no! anything, *anything* but that!' and she covers her face with her hands, moaning. 'And I—*I* have brought this curse upon him. I—I, who loved him!'

'You should have thought of that in time,' says Nurse Stirling, perhaps a little cruelly. 'Miss Heywood warned you, if you remember, at Rottingdean. Your answer to her was that he was a dastardly criminal, and that you could not rest until he was punished as he deserved, whatever you might feel afterwards. That was your wish, and the hand of God has smitten him. No earthly power can

97

cure him, but he may live for years—thirty, forty years perhaps; but he will never speak, will never move again. Whether he will be conscious of your presence, of course, no one can tell. Whether in total paralysis the mind is clear, the heart alive to suffer, is a point upon which, so far, science is dumb. For his own sake, let us hope, let us pray, that he is not; for in that case his sufferings would be too awful. Your place, Lady Hullingham, as his wife, is at his side. Miss Donati has left the house. I took upon myself, in your name, to send her off, and she left without a word before eight o'clock this morning. So you can return in all honour to your home, and take your place as mistress of the manor. Come, now; let us go to Sir Carlos. Poor fellow! Even I cannot help but pity him.'

The colour mounts for an instant to Mora's brow, and she presses Janet's arm with silent feeling.

By the library fire, in his easy-chair, the paralyzed man is sitting, with his silent, sphinx-like stare; and by his side another nurse is sewing. She rises as they enter, a sorrowful look on her honest, homely face.

'Lady Hullingham has come, and her nephew, Mr. Frank,' says Janet quietly. Then aside to Mora: 'Sir Thornton Bramwell sent Sister Joséphine this morning.

Lady Hullingham holds out her hand, with her fascinating smile.

'Thank you for coming, Sister Joséphine,' she says. 'I am as ignorant as a child about illness. Will you leave me with him, please?'

When she is alone, with a cry of agony she throws herself upon her knees by the stricken man, and takes his rigid hand, gazing wistfully into his staring eyes.

'Carlos! Carlos, my beloved! don't you know me, your little Mora?'
Silence!

'God! Oh, God! it isn't true? Carlos, say it isn't true! Will he never speak again?'

Never, Mora Hullingham—never again upon this earth.

There is no sign of recognition in the wide blue eyes, once so eloquent with their luminous fires. Mora is beside herself. She had never dreamed of a thing like this. True, she had wished him to suffer for his crime, had prayed that his soul might be wrung with remorse and wounded pride when the veil of hypocrisy fell from him; but that he should be stricken with such a doom as this! No! no! it is more than she can bear. Madly she paces up and down, and to and fro, beneath the pictured eyes of the woman she has avenged. Her soul is torn with anguish, and she cries aloud with bitter wailing:

'God, give him speech! give him speech again! Hear me, for Christ's sake, and give him speech!' and she wrings her hands above her head in the wildness of her cry.

No answer comes, no movement, to tell that the silent form is living. Suddenly an increase of pain in her side oppresses her, and her throat is burning with a dreadful fire. A creeping sensation of lassitude steals over her, and she feels the world go round.

'Am I ill?' she says, and then a deadly nausea takes hold of her, and she cries aloud: 'What has come to me? Carlos! Carlos! Help! Help me! I——'

Face downwards on the floor she falls, insensible. An hour or more goes by, but no one comes to succour her. They are afraid to intrude. At last young Hullingham peeps in, and is dismayed to find his aunt unconscious and prostrate upon the floor, near the man unable to lift a hand to help her.

With a sigh her nephew raises her, and gently lays her upon a couch. Then he goes to the door and calls to Nurse Stirling.

Mora opens her eyes, but they are burning with an unconscious light, and with the fires of fever.

'Adelaide! Adelaide!' she cries in delirium; 'of course you are not mad. Everybody knows you are not mad. Carlos shall save you—I will make him save you. He will never speak again, but he shall save you.'

'Send for the doctor, Mr. Hullingham, please,' says Janet.

Frank rings the bell and gives the message, and in a few minutes more a servant is galloping in the direction of the village.

'Put on more phosphorus,' goes on Mora in her wandering babble, while Frank and Nurse Stirling watch her anxiously. 'More! More phosphorus! It's not near luminous enough. There, now I shall do. Ha, ha, ha! I pity Carlos when he sees me!' and again her weird laugh rings out.

Great is the consternation in the servants' hall when they learn that both the master and 'Missie,' whom they so dearly love, are stricken down. Nurse Stirling, standing by Mora's couch, looks very stern. Her experience tells her what is wrong. Lady Hullingham grows worse and worse. Her distress of breathing is heartrending, as with bitter cries she clutches at her throat and side. And though her delirium is raving, her hands and limbs are icy with a clammy cold.

'What is it?' asks Frank in a breathless whisper. 'Seems like brain-fever, doesn't it?'

'The symptoms are not ordinary,' says Janet guardedly. Her lips are hard compressed, as always when deeply thinking.

In half an hour the doctor comes, glances at Sir Carlos, and nods to Janet, who introduces Frank.

Dr. Morecombe looks very grave as his eyes rest upon Mora.

'How long has she been like this?' he asks quickly of Nurse Stirling.

'She showed symptoms of a sudden illness last night, or, I should say, early this morning, for it was past midnight—symptoms which have grown steadily worse. The delirium has only supervened about an hour,' says Janet quietly.

'What were the premonitory symptoms?'

Nurse Stirling looks at Frank.

'Mr. Hullingham had best tell you that,' she says. 'I was not present.'

Frank, thus called upon, relates the condition of his aunt the night before, and also this morning, before the telegram summoned them to the Manor; and how he had discovered her insensible upon the floor.

'There appear to have been signs of decline for some months previous to this attack,' interposes Janet; and she tells of the patient's life of suffering and of exposure to wet and cold at the hand of her husband, Sir Carlos.

'H'm!' muses Dr. Morecombe sadly, as he strokes the heavy hair from Mora's brow; 'a sad case, truly—one of the most horrible it has been my lot to meet with. Knowing a part of this poor lady's history, it almost looks like a double retribution. Well, nurse, let's see what we can do for her! Little, I fear. Constitution undermined, and traces of a rapid decline; then last night's sudden seizure, with a tendency to fainting; pain in throat and side, delirium, without fever; heart's action impeded; distress of breathing, with stoppage of circulation. Nurse Stirling, you surely see what's wrong?'

'Yes; I saw it from the first.'

'Look here, Dr. Morecombe!' young Hullingham cries. 'For God's sake tell me what it is you fear! This suspense is unbearable!'

The doctor looks at him for one moment steadily without replying.

'Well, Mr. Hullingham, I regret to have to tell you that your aunt has taken poison,' he says at last.

'Merciful heavens! then it is true! Oh, my God!' Frank Hullingham cries wildly, turning white as death.

'What do you mean by that?' asks the doctor sternly, with a swift glance at the speaker.

'Before I answer you, tell me this, Dr. Morecombe: Can a person die from inhaling the fumes of phosphorus?'

The doctor starts.

'Most certainly he can, if he inhales much, for any length of time. Phosphorus is a most violent poison.'

'Then, Dr. Morecombe, my aunt is dying from phosphorus poison. Give her the antidote at once, and I'll tell you all about it.'

Sick at heart, and sorely puzzled by the young man's answer, the doctor turns to Nurse Stirling, and again he starts, for her face is pale, and she is striving to suppress some deep emotion.

Without appearing to notice it, he asks:

'Have you oil of turpentine in the house, nurse?'

'Mercifully, yes. Sister Joséphine has some in her medicine chest—I saw it this morning; and magnesia too. I fear it will be too late.' And she leaves the room.

Frank begins the story.

'A few weeks ago, Dr. Morecombe, my aunt, Lady Hullingham, commissioned me to purchase for her a few sticks of phosphorus, as she desired to make an experiment. Knowing that when at school, I and some other boys had frequently played pranks with phosphorus, I thought no harm, and got them for her.'

'She didn't state for what she required them?'

'No; but I discovered it last night for myself,' says Frank.

'How was that?' cries the doctor.

'Have you read in the papers to-day of the reception at Lady Mountjoy's house last night, Dr. Morecombe, and of the Phantom

Recital?' asks Frank, with apparent irrelevance.

'Yes; and I own it grieved me intensely,' the young doctor replies, glancing at the figure of Sir Carlos by the fire. 'But what, may I ask, has this to do with your aunt, Lady Hullingham?'—somewhat impatiently.

'Everything,' says Frank gravely. 'Aunt Mora was the reciter!'

'Good heavens!' cries the doctor, a light breaking in upon him at last. 'Go on; I begin to understand. She used phosphorus in the composition of her "make-up"?'

'Precisely. She wore a kind of Grecian drapery of some white stuff, and this was thickly coated with oil-diluted phosphorus, till in the coloured limelight she appeared as a spirit, clad in a misty, flaming vapour. I never saw anything so magnificent in my life; but it was most unearthly!'

'Poor creature! But what an insane idea!' the doctor cries. 'She might have set herself and the whole house in a blaze. Phosphorus is highly flammable. How long did she wear this gown?'

'In all, I should say about four hours.'

'Ah! Then there is no possibility of her recovery. I'm truly sorry for you, Mr. Hullingham;' for Frank has turned away.

'It's all my fault!' he cries passionately, as he walks to the window. 'I bought the infernal stuff, and I've killed her!'

'No, Frank, no,' comes from Mora's dying lips. She has regained her consciousness, and has heard his self-recrimination. 'If—you had—not got—it—I should have—procured it—some—other way.'

Nurse Stirling re-enters with the antidote. Lady Hullingham smiles. The doctor's finger is on her pulse, and as the nurse approaches he shakes his head.

'It's too late to save her life,' he says sadly; 'but we will give it to her, in order to have done our best.'

As he speaks, he forces a few drops of the turpentine mixture through her lips, which are already blue. She has sunk again into apparent coma, and her eyes, he sees, are filming with the film of death.

'She's poisoned with the fumes of phosphorus,' he says, with his hand upon her wrist. 'It's the gown at the Recital did it.' And he sighs.

'Was that dress made luminous with phosphorus?' cries Janet, appalled. 'She must have been mad! Why, every-one in the house might have been burnt! I thought it was Balmain's "luminous paint," which is harmless, or I should have forbidden it.'

'Well, it's too late for self-reproaches now,' says Dr. Morecombe. 'See, the end is near. She'll die in convulsions. Call Nurse Joséphine; we may want more help.'

For half an hour the wretched woman is racked in torment by the last terrible convulsive action of the poison, and it takes all the doctor's and the nurses' strength to hold her down. Frank Hullingham, watching the struggle from the window, is transfixed with horror.

At last the worst is over, and poor Mora sinks back exhausted upon the couch, when suddenly a spurious strength comes to her, and, with full consciousness in her dying hour, she struggles up, supported by the doctor and Nurse Stirling, and walks a step in the direction of Sr Carlos, by the fire. Frank advances to her and takes the doctor's place, putting his arm around her. For a moment, smiling, she lays her head upon his shoulder, but another spasm seizes her, and she screams.

'Mt side! Oh, the pain—the pain! My throat—burning! Give me water—water! Carlos, help me; I am—dying! I——'

She staggers forward a step; then, held by the doctor and the nurse, her eyes rest upon Adelaide's portrait. She pauses, her hand pressed to her left side. All wait in suspense for what may happen next. With a loud cry 'Adelaide! Adelaide—is—avenged!' she sinks down, and tenderly they bear her back to the couch.

She is dead.

*   *   *   *   *

Sir Carlos Hullingham lives on for years, tended by Sister Joséphine and his nephew Frank, until one day it is discovered he has passed away.

By Mora's side, in the great Hullingham vault, he is laid to rest.

May they both be pardoned, and rest in peace!

And thus to Patience Hullingham, the despised, insulted, is tardy justice done, for Reville's boy succeeds to the title and estates, and little Bertie—Sir Herbert Hullingham—is Master of the Manor.

THE END

Printed by BoD™in Norderstedt, Germany

9 781739 392161